Fit For Love

A WALL STREET TITAN NOVEL

ANNA ZAIRES

MISHA BELL

♠ MOZAIKA PUBLICATIONS ♠

Published by Mozaika Publications, an imprint of Mozaika LLC.
www.mozaikallc.com

Cover by Najla Qamber Designs
www.qamberdesignsmedia.com

ISBN: 978-1-63142-966-8
Paperback ISBN: 978-1-63142-970-5

PART ONE

Three Years Earlier

CHAPTER 1
Kendall

UGH, *why are men such dogs?*

Mr. Boss's Wife Number Five turns around, arching a trendily bushy eyebrow. "What did you say?"

Oh, crap. Did I say that out loud? I put on my most professional smile. "Nothing. Just—"

"What is that mopey face doing on my set?" Tierre vigorously fans himself with peacock feathers. "I told you, I can't have any negative juju here." He points his bejeweled finger into the distance, away from the dreadlocked white tiger, the albino iguana, and the giant mist machine working overtime—in other words, the usual things that make one think "high fashion." Or just "high."

I back away until I'm out of Mr. Boss's sight. It's my first week on the job, and I've already been in hot water twice—once for getting barked at by Tierre's female French bulldog (a bitch that is apparently hypersensitive to "sad juju vibes") and now again for somehow looking "mopey."

I mean, I do feel a bit sad and mopey. Or more than a bit, to be honest. I may have even cried in the bathroom on my lunch break yesterday. Which sucks because the cheating asshole I was dating doesn't deserve a single tear. Unless it's somebody tearing him a new one—a task for which I'd gladly volunteer.

I should probably just stop dating. Become a nun, stop waxing, and forget pedicures. Or worse, date total losers, like my friend Emma does. The guys she goes for could never get another girl of her caliber, so she's been spared the heartache of getting dumped by yet another hot dude. Or dumping *him* after finding out he was dating three other girls at the same time—which is my latest situation.

Whatever. I need to focus on de-mopefying myself... somehow. Maybe I should listen to some Bach? Meditate? Rewatch *Zoolander*?

"Hey, wait up," Wife Number Five says, catching up to me.

"Hey... you." I mentally kick myself for not writing down her name as soon as Mr. Boss introduced us. The problem is, a second later, he also introduced me to his dog, and as a result, I'm not sure which of them is Cleopatra and which is Catherine. The mnemonic for both is that there was a historical queen with the same name, but that only helps when it comes to not forgetting the names.

"Are you going through a breakup or something?" she asks.

Shit. The last thing I want is to have a girl talk with my boss's wife. Then again, if she sympathizes, maybe she'll ask her hubby to be nicer to me.

"I got cheated on," I admit.

She cocks her head. "And then?"

And then? "I dumped his ass." And I might've stuffed his favorite T-shirt into the garbage disposal and let it run.

"I see," she says sagely. "That's one of the many problems with the whole monogamy paradigm."

"Oh?" Please, for the love of God, don't invite me to an orgy—because that's where this seems to be headed.

"Not sure if you know this, but Tierre and I have an open marriage," she says, proudly lifting her surgeon-sculpted nose. "This way, cheating is impossible."

Is it? "That sounds really evolved," I say as nonjudgmentally as possible. "I'm just too possessive for that, I guess."

"You're just young," she says. "Your passions are running wild."

"Thanks?"

She's in her mid-forties to Tierre's sixty. Rumor has it, the gap between Mr. Boss and each wife gets wider with each iteration. Then again, also according to rumor, he may not be interested in women at all, except that he thinks a wife keeps people guessing at his sexual preferences and therefore gives him an air of mystery.

"Come closer," she says.

Reluctantly, I do—and it's like diving into a pool of perfume.

"I know exactly what you need," she whispers, leaning in.

"Oh?" *Seriously. Don't invite me to an orgy. I beg you.*

She pulls out a business card. Printed on it in neat letters is the word "Essence" and an address. "Go to this gym and ask for Ash," she says. "Thank me tomorrow."

Oh. A workout. That's a great idea. With enough endorphins in my body, I may look less mopey after all.

"Thanks." I pocket the card.

"No problem." She hands me her credit card, and when I glance at it, I see which of the two queen names is hers. "The first session is on me."

Does she realize she sounds like a drug dealer? "Thanks again, Catherine," I say earnestly. "I really appreciate it."

She waves that away. "I'm a good judge of character, and I think you're perfect for this job."

I feel like kissing her for saying that, but that's inappropriate, right? Not to mention, if I do kiss her, she may invite me to that orgy, so I just thank her gushingly instead and commit her name to permanent memory.

. . .

Emma calls me right as I finish telling my cabbie where I'm headed.

"Hey, Ems," I say. "How are things going?"

"The kittens are driving me insane," she says without missing a beat. "Especially the biggest one."

"That's Mr. Cottonball, right?"

I'm more of a dog person myself—at least when I'm not mad at men—but the kittens mean so much to my bestie that it's only polite to allow her to talk about them.

"Wrong," she says, and I can tell she's grinning without needing to see her. "The demon spawn's name is Mr. Puffs. Cottonball is actually an angel, and so is Queen Elizabeth."

Hmm. "If I were Cottonball, I'd be the one giving you shit for not bestowing me with any honorifics or titles."

She laughs and launches into a long story about something the kittens did, followed by several more. After about ten minutes, she must realize that even a saint would be losing interest in the subject, so she asks how things are with me. Sighing in relief, I tell her about my latest failure in the dating market.

"That really sucks," she says sympathetically. "After all the rotten luck you've had lately, you deserve a lucky break."

"Nope. No more getting lucky for me," I say firmly. "I'm done with men." And having kissed our mutual friend Janie back in college, I—unfortunately—have zero desire to bat for the other team.

Emma snorts. "Yeah, right. How long is that going to last? A week? Or—gasp—a month?"

"Listen, my darling," I say with an eyeroll. "Not all of us have an old lady's libido."

"Excuse me?" She huffs. "My libido is perfectly fine, thank you very much."

"Oh, yeah? When was the last time—"

"Kendall?" she says theatrically and hisses like a cat. "Kendall, can you hear me? I think I'm losing connection." She hisses again—though it might actually be one of her kittens this time.

"Seriously, Ems?"

Yep. She's dead serious. The sneaky little bitch hangs up on me, which is just as well because the cab stops at my destination.

WHEN I STEP INTO ESSENCE, I REALIZE IT'S A SOCIAL club for the uber rich that masquerades as a gym. Behind the front desk is a Warhol painting—a genuine one, I'm pretty sure—and in the far corner, I spot a celebrity heiress on an elliptical machine.

"Hello." I slide Catherine's card toward the supermodel-hot front desk woman. "I'm here to see Ash."

She looks flustered for a second but recovers quickly. "You will find clothes in the locker room." She gestures at the swanky entrance nearby. "Go and change, then warm up on that treadmill." She points to a machine near the heiress. "I'll have him find you there."

I head to the locker room as instructed, not surprised in the slightest when it turns out that the place provides you with activewear by Versace.

As I change, I make a mental note to find out if Tierre has ever dabbled in gym clothes and to suggest it in case he hasn't.

Exiting the locker room, I go to the treadmill in question and fiddle with the unfamiliar controls.

Soon, I'm running and generating those endorphins, but sadly, mopey thoughts intrude, so I bump up the speed, once. Twice. Thrice.

Crap. I never attached the red safety thingy to my leggings.

Well, better late than never. Panting, I grab the bar and reach for it—but just then, my right foot steps on the left.

Fuck me.

Instinctively, I let go of the bar as I fight to regain my balance, and that's a mistake because the belt carries me back in an eyeblink... and I find myself airborne.

CHAPTER 2

Ashton

A few minutes earlier

"ONE MORE," I order. "Good. Again."

Megan does three more crunches, and then, despite my strongest urging, she falls back on her mat.

"Get up," I say. "You have more in you."

"No, I don't." She pants until she catches her breath. "You know, I think you're more of a drill sergeant over video than in person. I thought that maybe—"

"Don't you want that six pack for your superheroine role?"

She nods sheepishly.

"Then do as I tell you. I'm here to help you accomplish what you want." I leave the obvious unsaid: If you don't like my training style, get a trainer who will pussyfoot around... and then suffer the consequences, of which the lack of a six pack would just be the start.

"No. I like your style." Her eyes gleam with mischief. "I guess I'm still not used to instructions like that... outside the bedroom."

I pretend I didn't hear the last bit. I don't date clients, not even if they're Hollywood sex symbols like Megan.

"Have you been following the meal plan?" I ask, mostly to change the topic.

She shakes her head. "My stomach has been cramping, and before you ask, it's not that time of the month."

I frown. "I might've given you too much fiber. Let me update the plan and shoot it over to you after you finish abs."

"Actually, I'm afraid we have to wrap up now," she says. "I have to get back to set."

I narrow my eyes at my phone screen. "Are you trying to get out of doing your reps?"

"No," she says with a slight eyeroll. "Do you want me to get a note from the producer?"

"No. But if this keeps up, I might just make you."

"Yes, sir." She gives me a mock military salute.

Strangely, I get that a lot from my clients. Maybe I should've joined the army. I toyed with the idea in high school, but my parents were strongly against it and I still listened to them at that point, so I went to college and then to business school—much to my regret.

I must be frowning because Megan says worriedly, "Hey, Ashton, I was just kidding. Please don't drop me as a client. I need that six pack, and you're the best person to get me there."

"Then follow the meal plan," I say gruffly. "And make sure we have an uninterrupted hour tomorrow."

"I will do that, I swear."

With that, she ends our video call.

I check my calendar. Today is a very light day. All I have left is a sparring session with my friend Marcus.

Good. This gives me a chance to browse the app store for a better way to help my clients when I'm not training them in person. What I'm looking for is an app that would let me track their progress while they're working out alone, and that would also have video capability—both for playing pre-recorded videos and for interactive sessions. Ideally, it should incorporate my meal plans, my sleep and hydration recommendations, as well as—

Someone places a hand on my shoulder. In an eyeblink, I'm on my feet, about to break the arm of the person who startled me.

"Jesus, chill," Gerald says.

Shit. I almost assaulted the owner of Essence and the person who's helped me greatly with my career.

"Sorry about that." I let go of his wrist and step back. "I tend to get jumpy when someone sneaks up on me."

No idea why that is, either. I think I was maybe born in the wrong place and time. With my violent reflexes, I would've made a great gladiator in Ancient Rome. Or a barbarian.

"No, I'm sorry," he says with a smirk. "I'll wear a bell next time."

"How can I help?" I smile broadly—a trick I use to put people at ease, especially after almost assaulting them.

Gerald smiles back. "I need a big favor."

"Sure. With what?"

Whatever it is, I doubt I can refuse. This gym has some unique equipment that I'd like to continue to have access to.

"Ash called in sick," Gerald says.

Wait a second. "Ash?"

"Asher," he says. "Don't worry. There's no other Ashton here."

"Which one is he? The short one?"

He sighs. "He's about your height. His distinguishing feature is that he's the least competent trainer here, so you covering for him will be a big upgrade for his clients."

"Hey, I was going to help you even without smoke up my ass," I say. "But with it, I'll even allow his clients to call me Ash—and you know how much I hate shortening my name."

"So far it's *a* client," he says. "Singular."

"Ah. Okay. Where is he?"

He gestures toward the cardio machines by the entrance. "*She* is on the third treadmill on the right. Brown hair. Pretty. Her name is Kendall."

Pretty? Another one? I've recently decided that I prefer to work with less attractive female clients because that makes it easier to follow my self-imposed "no sleeping with clients" rule.

Oh, well.

"All right," I say. "I've got it from here."

"Thanks."

He leaves, and I head toward Kendall.

And... fuck me. Thanks to the mirrors all over the place, the closer I get, the better I can see her from the front and back—and I realize that Gerald calling this woman "pretty" was an understatement of sperm whale proportions.

She is not merely pretty.

She is beautiful.

No. Gorgeous. With her long, sleek dark hair sweeping from side to side, she looks like she's running toward a shampoo commercial. The borrowed leggings and tank top worn by every other woman at this gym look both stylish and effortless on her. They hug her tight, perfect body in all the right places, and with the small beads of sweat glistening on her smooth skin, nothing can stop the X-rated images circling through my mind.

Are her nipples showing through her top? If it were up to me, I would take her back to my place right now and—

A spike of adrenaline cuts down on my musings as I notice Kendall fumbling for the safety tether. And then... Shit!

She takes flight.

I leap forward as my martial arts training kicks in.

Landing next to her treadmill, I spread my arms.

She smashes vertically into my embrace.

Reflexively, I cradle her against me, all her soft parts a perfect fit with my hard ones. Which, to my shock, get much, much harder as blood surges through my veins and primal awareness of her envelops my senses. I'm sharply cognizant of everything about her—her slender curves... her feminine scent, a mixture of apple and hibiscus, with a hint of something ineffable that's purely her... the way she's panting and trembling, as if I've just made her come...

Which I very much want to do, over and over again, with my tongue, and my hands, and my cock.

My inner barbarian is already scouting nearby surfaces, like the bench to my left and the yoga mats in the corner and—

"Thank you," she says breathlessly, her hazel eyes glued to mine.

"You're welcome." I keep holding her against me, as though if I let go, she'll continue her terrifying trajectory to the floor.

"Seriously." She moistens her pink, soft-looking lips. "You can let go of me now."

Ah.

Right.

With great reluctance, I set her on her feet and step back. The fog of lust is slowly clearing from my brain, leaving room for other emotions—like anger.

What the fuck was she thinking, being so careless?

She could've gotten badly hurt.

I could've not caught her in time.

She could've been—

"Aren't you going to say something?" She blinks her long, sooty eyelashes at me.

"Yes," I grit out. "Don't you ever, ever, do something like that again. Is that understood?"

CHAPTER 3
Kendall

A few seconds earlier

AS I FLY from the treadmill, time seems to slow, giving me a cruel opportunity to picture myself breaking a limb. Or my neck. Or my tailbone. Either way, I will be so full of negative juju Tierre will fire me for sure.

Assuming I survive.

To my huge surprise, I don't hit the ground.

Instead, I land upright, smashing into something hard yet pliant and enveloping at the same time.

Something that smells deliciously masculine.

Realizing my eyes are squeezed shut, I open them and... holy fuck.

My savior is built like a Greek statue but with more muscles. His sun-kissed hair is a couple of inches too long, a surfer's look. Only instead of the ocean, he smells like lime zest, clean skin, and toe-curling sex.

Speaking of sex, his blue-gray eyes are hooded, and I can feel something big and hard against my belly. Something that is definitely not a flashlight.

"Thank you," I manage to say, albeit a bit breathlessly. I'm really hoping Mr. McScrumptious can't feel my drumming heartbeat or my pebbled nipples.

"You're welcome," he murmurs in a deep, soft voice that reminds me of melted things—like caramel, hearts, and panties.

With effort, I pull myself together—not an easy task since he's still holding me. Since he didn't get the hint from my thank-you, I say, "Seriously, you can let go of me now."

I guess I could also push him away, but I'm not sure I can bring myself to do it—not with all the jolts of sensual energy zapping through my body, leaving gooseflesh in their wake.

Sadly, he listens to me and lets me go.

Grr. Why did I insist on that? I could've enjoyed his embrace for a few more minutes before it would've seemed too weird... right?

He even steps away—and the idiot that I am, I immediately miss his proximity.

As he stands there, his gorgeously carved face goes through a series of expressions, settling on something dark, which, for some reason, only makes me want to jump back into his arms—or into his bed.

Crap. *Focus, Kendall. You've sworn off men, remember?*

I swallow and pull myself together, again. "Aren't you going to say something?"

Between the silence and his dark expression, I'm starting to feel all kinds of uncomfortable, and not all of it down south.

"Yes," he growls. "Don't you ever, ever, do something like that again. Is that understood?"

My hackles—which I thought I'd lasered off a long time ago—rise. "Ex-fucking-cuse me?"

A muscle in his jaw ticks. "How could you have been so careless? You could've hit your head."

What the fuck? Who the hell does he think he is?

"If I had, I'd still be smarter than you," I retort caustically.

He blows out a breath. "Is it that hard to attach the safety key?"

So that's what the thingy is called? "I didn't realize I had to. I usually run on the street."

His eyes narrow dangerously. "The street?"

Is he picturing me running through Manhattan traffic? What kind of an idiot does he take me for?

"I run in the park," I clarify. "'On the street' is just a turn of phrase."

"Which park?" he demands. "Some are worse than the street."

"East River. Not that it's any of your business."

Seriously, what is up with this guy?

He cocks his head. "I'm your fitness trainer, so anything to do with you running is my business."

"Wait. You're Ash?"

For some reason, I expected someone more boring-looking. Not to mention dressed in the gym's uniform instead of short shorts that expose his powerful legs and a tank top that shows enough lickable skin to make one salivate.

He grimaces. "You can call me Ash if you insist, but I prefer to go by—"

"Don't worry, I won't be calling you anything. This whole thing was a mistake. I'm just going to leave."

He crosses his arms over his impressive chest. "Do you want a trainer who'd let you break your arms? Your neck?"

I roll my eyes. "What I want is a rush of endorphins to cheer me up. This—whatever you're doing—is accomplishing the opposite."

"You came for endorphins?" he asks, and the gleam in his eyes tells me he's picturing a completely different endorphin-generating scenario from the one I meant.

And there I go again. My panties are officially damp.

"This conversation is over." I turn to leave, as much to get his perfect face out of my sight as to make a statement.

"Wait," he says—and fuck, his voice alone is doing things to my insides. He steps around me to block my way. "If you don't want a session with me, let me at least show you a few machines that can help you get those endorphins."

What he seems to leave unsaid is that these

machines are the second-best way to get endorphins when he's involved. The number one way is, of course, to fuck his brains out. Or is it my brains?

Also, why is "brains" plural in that expression?

I give him my best glare. "You really think I can't use a machine without your supervision?"

He smirks, and damn him, it's a sexy smirk. "Use safely? I think we just saw the answer to that."

I resist the urge to growl. "You're insufferable. What happened was a freak accident, nothing more."

"If you say so." He pointedly glances at the cursed treadmill.

"Let me show you how little I need your so-called help." I stomp over to the nearest machine—an upright bench with two paddle-like things at waist level. I have no idea what it does, but there are instructions on it, and I learned how to read when I was five.

"That one?" He arches his eyebrow in an infuriatingly cocky way. "You sure you don't want to make your point somewhere else?"

"Stop following me. Or shut up."

"This should be interesting." He folds his arms across his chest again and watches me, eyes gleaming with amusement.

I read the small font.

Sit upright, with back against the pad.

Hmm. As I plop onto the seat, the paddle thingies align with my legs, which I should have expected but somehow didn't. This gives me an unpleasant suspicion, like maybe I've seen this exercise before, on a less fancy machine and—

"Hip abduction?" he murmurs. "Interesting."

I turn from the instructions to glare at him, but it's a mistake, insofar as I get ensnared by his ridiculously handsome looks again. "Abduction is not hip, no matter how cool the aliens."

He snorts. "Hip as in those that don't lie in that song by Shakira." He gestures at his own narrow hips, but that just draws my attention to the nearby bulge in his shorts. "As to abduction, it means your limbs will move *away* from your midsection. Both words are homonyms, but I bet you knew that."

I snort. "I don't know what a homonym is, but it sounds vaguely homophobic."

It also sounds like Ash might've gone to college and/or read a book, which makes him impossibly more attractive.

Crap. Even his exasperated sigh is sexy.

"Go on then," he says after said sigh. "Let's see if you're as smart with this machine as you are with your mouth."

Is that his way of asking me for a blowjob?

No. It's a challenge, so I read the rest of the instructions… and my heart sinks. My earlier suspicion was correct. This is that machine where you push apart the paddles with your knees to end up with your legs spread, like you're begging someone to fuck you—or summoning a gynecologist.

Usually, in an empty gym or if surrounded by women, I wouldn't have a problem spreading my legs, no matter how obscenely wide. But to do so with Ash staring, and while I'm so wet…

"Nope." I leap to my feet. "There will be no abductions today."

He smiles—and it's like a glorious sunrise after a hurricane. "I can show you a better way to work those same muscles, using movements that are more natural."

"Oh, yeah? Let me see this alleged way."

He leads me to a machine with cables sticking out of it and grabs two thingies that look suspiciously like a collar a sub would wear in BDSM—with a metal ring attached and everything.

Is this workout about to turn kinky? And… do I want it to?

"You put these around your ankles," he says, demonstrating on himself.

He then clips the ring on the collar—or shackle—to the cable on the bottom of the machine, which still looks kind of kinky now that my mind has gone there. With four of these shackles, two on wrists and two on ankles, one could be restrained in a spread-eagle position and then—

"Next, you do this." He extends his bound leg to the side, lifting the weight attached to the cable.

Fuck me. All his muscles—but especially those in his powerful legs—flex in the process of this demonstration, doing damage to my sanity and panties.

"And then with the other leg." He clips his other ankle in and stands with his back to me, giving me a view of his perfectly sculpted back and ass.

"Now." He frees himself from the shackles and hands them to me. "Your turn."

CHAPTER 4
Ashton

FUCKING FUCK. Finding a client attractive is bad. Getting hard for a client is infinitely worse.

The problem is, knowing something is bad for me doesn't change anything, especially when it comes to my dick. Since meeting Kendall, I've gotten hard at the slightest provocation—like when I pictured her spreading her legs on that machine. And I'm hard now, with this much tamer exercise. I find every detail of her movements erotic. Even the way she holds the metal bar of the functional trainer makes me think "stripper pole." It doesn't help that the muscles involved with this exercise include the *gluteus medius* and *minimus*, which are located in her tight, round ass.

Oh, and did I mention I'm wearing shorts? Stupid. Had I known what would be in store for me, I would've worn my bulkiest cargo pants, and maybe the cup that I use during sparring.

Speaking of sparring, since Kendall's back is turned

to me, I get my phone out and shoot Marcus a text, warning him I might not be able to make it to our session.

When I look up from my phone, Kendall is done with her exercise and glaring at my hands. "Am I boring you?"

I put my phone away and grin at her. "I thought you didn't want my help."

"Yeah, well, now that you've forced said help on me, you might as well act professional."

Me, unprofessional?

I grit my teeth, then tell myself not to engage. She's clearly baiting me. "Your form was perfect throughout, so I doubt I missed anything by not monitoring the last few reps."

My phone dings in my pocket.

She lifts an eyebrow. "Are you going to check that?"

"No." I bet it's a reply from Marcus. "I can do it after."

"Is that any way to treat your girlfriend?" she asks, and flushes immediately.

Interesting.

"I don't have a girlfriend." I give her a mocking smile when her flush deepens. "What about your boyfriend? How does he feel about you asking other guys about their relationship status?"

Her pretty lips purse together. "I don't have a boyfriend. Men are dogs."

"Surely not *all* men?"

Did some asshole make her feel this way?

If he were here, I'd round-kick him in the jaw.

"Fine, *most* men are dogs," she concedes. "A rare few, like my dad, aren't."

It must be nice to say that about one's dad. "Thank you," I say smoothly, pushing the thought away.

She snorts. "Oh, 'most' absolutely includes *you*."

I give her a level look. "As a dog parent, I don't actually consider that an insult. Dogs are famous for their loyalty."

"Dogs hump everything," she says pointedly.

"When I commit to a woman, I don't even look at anyone—or anything—else."

I have no idea why I just told her that, even though it's the absolute truth.

She doesn't look like she believes me. "Oh, really? Will you offer up a bridge for me to buy as well? Sign me up for a multi-level marketing scheme?"

Scratch that. I do know why I told her that. I'm dying to fuck her, and she doesn't look like the type to indulge in a one-night stand. The only way into her pants is for her to see me as a dating prospect. Not that I date clients. Then again...

"On a completely unrelated note," I say casually. "Am I right in assuming you don't want me as your trainer?"

She nods. "Today's session was a gift. I can't afford this gym or the services of a trainer—but if I could, I wouldn't hire *you*."

I clutch my chest theatrically. "That was a low blow."

"Hey, some people might want an overbearing know-it-all for a trainer, but I sure don't."

Hmm. "If your session was a gift, I should point out that this place doesn't do refunds."

"So?"

"So maybe you should let me teach you some exercises that you can do at home. That way, you can get your endorphins for free."

This is actually a long-term goal of mine: to bring fitness to people who can't afford me. But in the short term, I'd be satisfied if I could optimally help the select few who *can* afford me. An app would be really useful to that end. My clients travel a lot, and simple videoconferencing has too many limitations.

She eyes me dubiously. "Can you do it without bossing me around?"

"Sure."

Because I'll teach her bodyweight exercises where she's as likely to get hurt as when getting out of bed.

Fuck. Thinking of beds in her vicinity is not good for my equilibrium. As I begin to demonstrate the different variations of planks, things only get harder from there—pun intended. I've never realized how much certain exercises resemble sexual positions. Especially knee planks, both with straight and bent arms. But the worst is probably the reverse plank because of how it pushes up her small, perky breasts.

The torture of my dick continues during pushups and persists all the way through to lunges and squats.

"That's it," she says after a second set of squats. "I can't do this anymore."

Usually, I'd chastise a client for wanting to give up so quickly, but Kendall isn't my client. Not to mention, I don't think I could watch her thrust out her booty in another rep without my balls bursting into a blue cloud.

"All right," I say as professionally as I can. "You did really well, and if you do what I've showed you regularly, you'll get all the endorphins you need—plus your bones and muscles will be stronger than ever."

"Right. Well… thanks." She swipes the back of her hand over her glistening forehead. "This wasn't as bad as I thought it might be."

"You're welcome." I debate if I should ask her for her number or provide mine, but I don't think she's ready for that yet.

No. A more Machiavellian approach is needed.

"It was a pleasure meeting you, Kendall," I say with exaggerated politeness. "I wish you luck with all your future endeavors."

The only thing that gives me the strength to walk away from her and back to the men's locker room is the knowledge that, unbeknownst to her, we'll be meeting again shortly.

I'M CHANGING QUICKLY WHEN I GET A CALL FROM Marcus, who sounds annoyed that I didn't reply to his last text.

"I was with a client," I say. "Sorry about canceling. I'll have to kick your ass some other time."

And I truly am sorry. Despite his riches, Marcus takes little joy in life, so sparring with me is probably the highlight of his week.

"How about we see whose ass gets kicked tomorrow afternoon?" Marcus says. "Assuming that fits into your oh-so-busy schedule."

"Tomorrow works. But are you really giving me shit about the one time I have a work conflict? You do this to me all the fucking time."

"It's happened three times," Marcus retorts. "And once, you only thought we had a session, but we did not."

He's keeping score? Why am I not surprised? Attention to detail is one of the many skills that have helped my friend score billions of rich people's money to manage in his fund.

"Fine. You've canceled three times, and I've only done it once," I say. "So I can move two more sessions before you have the right to—"

Fucker. He hung up on me. But hey, in the time it took to have that conversation, he probably missed a chance to make a few million. So I guess we're even.

Not for the first time, I wonder what it would be like if I were as rich as my parents have always pushed me to be. On the one hand, I could hire a Mexican food truck to follow me around all day, so I could get tacos whenever I want. But then my parents would learn about my success and be all "see, we told you to do that," and that would suck ass. I know they wish for a son who's more like Marcus. Unfortunately, they have me.

Maybe if they'd been no-good alcoholics like Marcus's mom, I would've had some of his ambition. Then again—

Shit. Kendall. I have to hurry.

Tying my laces, I make my way outside and wait for my quarry to appear.

CHAPTER 5
Kendall

IT TAKES me a few seconds to realize Ash just walked away without asking me out.

What the actual fuck?

He didn't ask for my number either. Or give me his. Or—

Wait, do I wish he'd done any of those things?

No way. But it would've been great for my bruised ego.

Asshole. I bet he knew I'd turn him down, so he didn't bother. Then again, he doesn't seem like the kind of guy who would have a problem handling rejection—not when he can crook a finger at any female in his vicinity and she'd come running. Come to think of it, is it possible he's never been rejected? If so, maybe he didn't want to know what that feels like.

As I change in the locker room, I dwell on this topic and decide that the reason I'm so upset is that I was confident he would ask me out.

I mean, why else check if I were single, right?

That's like leading a woman on.

Damn it.

Enough.

"Excuse me," I say to one of the cleaners when she enters the locker room. "What do I do with the dirty clothes?"

"Throw away the socks and put the rest in here." She points at a large hamper nearby.

Throw away the socks? Score! That means I can also keep them, so not everything is going to shit today. I walk over to a roll of plastic bags meant for wet swimwear and take one.

When I get back to my locker, I take off the socks and store them carefully in the bag, making sure to seal it tightly in order to lock in the smell. Stashing the bag in my purse, I drop the rest of my workout clothes in the designated hamper and walk through the gym with my head held high, looking for a certain someone in my peripheral vision.

Nope. He's not training anyone else or working out by himself.

I guess that's it.

I exit through the fancy doors onto the street and head in the direction of the subway station instead of taking another cab.

There. I can be economical too. Maybe I should text Emma and give her an update, both on the workout and on my bout of thriftiness. She thinks I'm a frivolous spender and that my parents pay for everything, but the latter couldn't be further from the truth.

Wait a second. Is it serendipity, or is that a Manolo Blahnik store appearing out of thin air just as I've saved some money?

Yep. It's a sign. I turn to head toward it—and run smack into a wall of familiar muscles that gives my whole body a zippy tingle.

"Now that's a pretty literal interpretation of 'bumping into someone you know,'" Ash says with a grin as I awkwardly push away. "Where are you headed in such a hurry?"

"Subway," I lie, not willing to get into the subject of shoes or, relatedly, socks. The latter is not something I ever talk about with people.

He looks around. "Subway the sandwich place or the train?"

"The train." I gesture vaguely in the direction of the station.

"Great," he says. "That's where I'm headed as well. Mind if I tag along?"

"This is a public street in a free country." I head in the direction of the station, and he falls into step next to me, his strides long and confident.

I try not to stumble over my feet. I'm viscerally aware of his tall, powerfully built body next to me, so much so my heart races and my palms sweat.

It's like I'm a teen on her first-ever date with a boy. A skinny, geeky teen with braces who plays the sousaphone in the marching band.

Yeah, not going there.

"You mentioned being a dog parent," I say, desperate for a distraction. "What kind of dog are we talking about?"

"Tricky question. I foster whenever I can, but I also have a corgi rescue who lives with me on a permanent basis." He hands me his phone that displays a picture of an adorable short-legged pup. "His name is Sir Eats-Minced-Meat-a-Lot, or Ems for short."

I almost drop his phone. "I have a friend named Emma, and I call her Ems too."

As he takes his cell back, our fingers brush, and the resulting tingle makes me momentarily dizzy and breathless. "I knew we would find something in common," he murmurs, slanting me a glance. "Though I didn't expect it would be this."

I try to get my breathlessness under control. "Did I mention that she's a cat person? I think that makes it worse."

He stops, his face twisted in mock horror. "Don't tell me you're a cat person as well."

"I think I prefer canines to felines."

"Whew," he says and resumes walking. "I was just about to cross the street."

"Don't be too happy." My lips twist in an involuntary smile. "The margin of said preference is tiny."

"That's because you haven't met a dog like Ems—or Sir Ems, as I'll call him from now on, to avoid confusion."

I smile wider. "Sir Ems? That has a very noble ring to it."

"Corgis are very popular with British royalty. So that part makes perfect sense."

"Shouldn't he be Lord Ems then?"

He laughs, and the resulting sound does to my ears what his touch did to my skin. "Sorry to change the topic," he says, his voice still filled with amusement, "but have you ever been to that place?" He gestures at a charming coffee shop a few feet away.

I shake my head.

"I want to go there. Do you want to join me?" He accompanies the question with a panty-dropping smile. "They have the best espresso in the city."

My heart starts racing like I've already imbibed a gallon of espresso. "The best in the city? That's a bold statement."

He nods sagely. "Let me get one for you, so you can decide if it's worth that honor."

"Okay." Crap. Did I just agree to a date?

He leads me to the place, and it turns out to be the kind of fancy café where you have to sit down and order the coffee from a menu. Or, more accurately, this is a French bistro that serves hot drinks and pastries alongside savory foods such as Croque Madame and Croque Monsieur.

"What can I get you to drink?" asks the waiter without even a hint of a French accent.

"Chamomile," I say almost at the same time as Ash says, "Mint tea."

"Sure." The waiter hands us menus and leaves.

As soon as we're alone, Ash arches an eyebrow. "I thought you wanted coffee."

"I thought you did too."

"Nope. I told you that I was headed here, and that they have the best espresso in the city. You *assumed* I wanted to drink it, but you know what they say about that word."

I narrow my eyes. "Something about asses, me, and you?"

"Your ass got a good workout today."

"No thanks to you being an ass."

"Sticks and stones."

"Why don't you want coffee?" I suspect it's the same reason for both of us, but I don't want to "assume."

He gestures at the large clock on the wall. "I don't consume caffeine after five."

Yep. "Me neither. Not unless I want to be up all night long."

"All. Night. Long." His eyes heat up. "If I change my order, will you?"

Is that an innuendo? "I'm sticking with chamomile. I'll need its calming properties if I'm to spend any more time in your company."

"Below the belt, again." He opens the menu. "And this after we've found a second thing we seem to have in common."

My stomach rumbles before I can reply.

He flashes his white teeth in a grin. "A good workout can work up an appetite."

I open the menu in sullen silence and scan everything, unsure of what I want.

"I've had the ratatouille here," he says. "And the vegetable crêpe. Both were delicious."

I look up. "Are you vegan or something?"

If so, it's odd that he didn't tell me about it in the first five seconds of our acquaintance.

"I just like nutritious food, which means eating a lot of vegetables."

Well then… "If I get a crêpe, it will be with triple cheese, double every meat, and zero veggies."

I say it just to needle him. I actually like vegetables and eat pretty healthy myself.

He shrugs. "What you order is your prerogative. You're not my client, and you didn't ask me to help you eat better."

The waiter comes back with our teas. "Do you know what you want to order?"

Ash gets the ratatouille, and despite what I said a second ago, when I order my crêpe, I ask for just one layer of cheese, a single meat, and *fines herbes*.

"Aren't herbs vegetables?" Ash asks as soon as we're alone again. "If so, you have more than zero veggies in your dish."

"No," I say firmly. "You only use a little bit of an herb, but a lot when it's a vegetable."

He smirks. "So… if someone eats only a little bit of say, spinach, for them, it becomes an herb?"

Damn him. Now I want spinach in my crêpe.

"Excuse me," I say before chasing after the waiter to

adjust my order.

When I come back, Ash looks like the cat who ate the canary—which tells me he definitely overheard me with the waiter.

"I have a craving for spinach," I mumble.

His smirk widens. "I take full credit for that. It's only been a short time, but I'm already a good influence on you. Spinach has a ton of vitamin K, which, among other things, helps with coagulation."

"Coagulation, as in ability to heal wounds? Are you planning to cut me or something?"

He chokes on his mint tea. "That got dark quickly."

I blow on my chamomile. "It's a risk you take when you squabble about definitions."

"You asked if herbs were vegetables, not me." He sets his cup down. "I have a better dilemma for you. Isn't the crêpe you ordered basically a quesadilla?"

Huh. "No, a quesadilla is closer to a grilled cheese. Next thing you'll be asking is whether tacos are sandwiches."

He gasps. "Tacos are not sandwiches… but hot dogs are tacos, for sure."

I snort. "And Pop-Tarts are a type of calzone."

He rewards me with that devastating smile of his. "Coffee is bean soup if you think about it. Cereal is also soup, or maybe even a smoothie?"

My stomach rumbles again. "Crêpes are thin pancakes."

"Pizza is an unfolded taco."

Before I can come up with more, the waiter comes back with the ratatouille.

"Want to try it?" Ash asks.

If I succumb to temptation, this will feel even more like a date. Then again, I'm starving, so I can't help snatching a bite. Nor can I help the moan that escapes my lips as the delicious flavors explode on my tongue.

When I open my eyes—which I didn't realize were closed—Ash is looking at me with a peculiarly intense expression.

I clear my throat. "Is ratatouille a stew or a casserole? And if it is a stew, is it essentially a thick soup and therefore a type of smoothie?"

Before Ash can answer, my crêpes arrive.

When we're alone again, I taste the crêpes, and another moan escapes my lips.

"That good?" he asks, staring at my mouth.

I nod enthusiastically. "Want a taste?"

"Yes." His eyes glint dangerously. "I really want a taste."

Not sure what possesses me to do it, but I cut a piece, and instead of putting it on his plate like a sane person, I feed it to him, as if we were role-playing an emperor and his concubine.

Holy crap. Watching a guy chew and swallow should not be this arousing. Except it is. So much so that I wonder how crazy it would be if I were to suggest we take this food to go and head over to my place.

No. Way too crazy. Even if this is a date, it would be

our first, and I don't have sex until I get to know a person.

"Delicious," he murmurs.

I blow on my chamomile tea again. My plan is to gulp down the tea as soon as it cools and pray that it calms my overactive libido. Clearly, just reminding myself that men are dogs isn't cutting it anymore.

"So," he says. "Tell me a little bit about yourself."

That makes it official. This *is* a date.

"Like what?" I ask, my heart pounding at the realization.

He shrugs. "Do you have any siblings?"

"Yeah. An older brother, Cameron. He's the reason boys were afraid to ask me out in high school." At least that's what I tell myself because it's better than the other possibility: that no one wanted to date the awkward geek from the marching band. "How about you?"

He smiles. "A younger sister, Jordan. She probably has the same complaint about me that you have about your brother, but in my defense, I've only beaten up one of her boyfriends, and the asshole deserved it."

If Jordan had boyfriends, plural, then it's not like my situation at all, but I'm not admitting that.

"Are you a native New Yorker?" I ask.

I feel like he isn't, but I'm not sure why.

"Nope. What about you?"

I shake my head. "I grew up in Connecticut."

His eyes twinkle. "Why do people from Connecticut

always give their state as the place where they're from?"

I roll my eyes. "And where are *you* from?"

"Boston. Notice how I didn't say 'Massachusetts.'"

That tracks. He doesn't have the signature accent, but something must've given him away. "When I tell people I grew up in Berlin, they assume I'm talking about the one in Germany, not Connecticut."

"Ich falle aus allen Wolken," he says.

I narrow my eyes. "Did you just put a curse on me in German?"

He grins. "It means, 'I didn't expect that' or something similar. The literal translation is 'I fall from all clouds.'"

Huh. "You're German?"

"No. I'm a European mutt, with maybe one percent German blood—if that. But I did take German back in college."

So he did go to college. Called it.

"What about you?" he asks.

"I'm also a mutt. According to a DNA test, I have some Russian, Native American, English, German, and Irish in me."

"Do you know any other languages?"

"I took Spanish in school, but don't ask me to say anything."

He flashes a white grin. "I wouldn't be so cruel."

Damn it. He's done nothing sensual in the last minute, nor has he said anything profound, but I'm falling deeper and deeper into this romantic rabbit hole of a date.

Grabbing my now-cooled chamomile tea, I gulp it in desperation.

This is it.

I see two unequal options playing out in front of me. One—the less likely—is that this tea will magically calm me down.

The other—and way more likely—is that I'll end up in his bed by the end of the night.

CHAPTER 6

Ashton

WHEN I WAITED for Kendall outside the gym, I was confident I'd be able to coax her to go on a date with me, but I had no idea I'd have such a great time on said date.

Or that I'd be this fucking turned on.

No. Scratch that. The latter doesn't surprise me, not after that workout.

"You mentioned college," she says. "What did you major in?"

Fuck. This isn't my favorite topic. "My undergraduate degree is in economics."

No. Wait. Why did I say "undergraduate?" Obviously, she'll—

"You went to grad school as well?"

She sounds impressed, and I only have myself to blame.

"Business school," I admit reluctantly. "But I'm taking a break from it."

"Taking a break" sounds better than "dropped out of my MBA program," right?

She cocks her head. "When are you going back to it?"

My smile is forced. "You sound like my parents," I say, trying to keep it light.

I should've guessed she'd be one of those women who think being a personal trainer is not a real job.

Even in the gym uniform, she looked like a million bucks. Dressed in street clothes, she's the epitome of high fashion, one of those effortlessly stylish women you encounter in the Hamptons or on the Upper West Side. Or in my parents' circle—but that's not an association I want to have with her.

Either way, she probably dates investment bankers, doctors, and lawyers, not gym trainers like myself.

Kendall must pick up on some tension because she winces and says, "Sorry, didn't mean to touch a sore spot."

I shrug and take a deep breath, ready to change the subject. "What about you? What was your major?"

I don't bother asking if she's gone to college. Everything about her screams it.

"Fashion design," she says. "And I just applied for an MFA program in the same thing."

"You want to be a fashion designer?"

She certainly dresses the part.

Her eyes glint excitedly. "I do. Fashion can be so transformative, don't you think?"

I don't, but... "Fitness can be similarly

transformative. People think it's all about the body, but so much of it is really about the mind and self-confidence."

She all but bounces in her seat. "Exactly!"

I want to kiss her, badly. It's an urge that's been growing since the moment she landed in my arms, and I can no longer resist. Calling forth every ounce of my charm, I lean forward and pitch my voice low. "What are you doing after this?"

Her eyes widen, and a pretty blush creeps up her smooth cheeks. "I was... I—" She fumbles for her cup just as her bag drops off her chair.

She whips around, presumably to catch it, only to knock into a passing waiter carrying a tray with soup. I spring into action, reaching across the table to pull her out of harm's way, but this time, I'm not fast enough.

The bowl tips over and directly onto her chest, covering her whole outfit in creamy liquid.

Fuck! "Are you hurt? Was that hot?" I demand.

She looks at me, her eyes wild. "No. It's cold."

Whew. "Thank God they forgot to warm it."

"No one forgot anything," the waiter says defensively. "It's vichyssoise. It's supposed to be served chilled."

I glare at him. "Are you sure you should be talking?"

"You're right," the guy says meekly. "I'm so sorry. Needless to say, your meal is on us."

Turning away before I give in to the temptation to smack him, I grab our table napkins and dab at the mess, at least until I realize that I'm much too close to Kendall's perfect breasts, especially for a public place.

"Here." I hand her the napkins. "Use these."

She takes them with a sigh, only to toss them onto the table after a few seconds of fruitless dabbing. "It's like cleaning a football field with a Q-Tip."

She's got a point. The thick soup covers her so thoroughly she'd need to run through a carwash to get clean.

"How about we swing by my place?" I suggest. "It's across the street. You can borrow something of mine to get home." And the fact that she'll have to give the clothes back is an excuse for us to meet again.

She narrows her eyes. "Earlier, you said you had to take the subway to get home."

Busted… but wait. "I never said I was headed home. Just to the subway. I could've been going to the Met or MoMA."

"Both are already closed," she says. "Try a better lie."

"A stroll in Central Park? A Broadway show?"

"Why do all those things sound like dates?" She stands up, and globs of viscous white liquid drip onto the floor.

I grin ruefully. "Maybe because I was brainstorming where to take you the next time?"

She gestures at the mess. "I look like I've been on a bukkake porn film set, yet you still want there to be a next time?"

Fuck me. I didn't make the connection before, but it

does look like she's covered in cum… which naturally makes me want to cover her in mine.

With effort, I wrench my mind away from those images. "So… do you want to change?"

She nods. "Lead the way."

Though our meal is supposed to be comped, I throw some cash on the table on the way out.

As we cross the street and enter the elevator in my building, I tell her stories about the silly excuses I've heard from clients for why they don't want to work out, like "I'm going to the bar tonight, so I won't make our one p.m. appointment tomorrow," or "My dog had an upset stomach, and I ended up walking her so much that I don't need any more exercise."

"Is that what I'm going to be?" she asks as we approach the door to my apartment. "A story about how a client fell off the treadmill and got covered in soup?"

"No." Hopefully, this will be the "how I met you mother" story that I tell our kids.

Wait, what? Kids? Where did that insane thought come from?

Minutes ago, I was contemplating a one-night stand… and now, reproduction?

One way or another, I need to get this woman out of my head before I do something stupid. If my short and disastrous relationship with Gwyneth taught me anything, it's that I'm not ready for a serious commitment. Not anytime soon.

Shit. Now that I've thought of Gwyneth, I realize

that Kendall reminds me a bit of her—at least insofar as she is also the type of woman my parents would love and therefore push me toward.

"Jeesh, that was just a joke," Kendall says. "You don't need to get all serious."

Fuck. "Sorry. You just made me realize that I should have something like trainer-client confidentiality, like shrinks do."

I unlock the door to the sound of happy barking and grin as Ems looks up at me with his intelligent eyes, wags his tail for all he's worth, and gives me a doggy grin.

"How are you doing, bud?" I ask.

He wags his tail harder.

"You've been knighted," I tell him. "Henceforth, you're Sir Ems. You may rise."

He cocks his head in confusion, but Kendall laughs, which is when Sir Ems becomes aware of her for the first time and showers her feet with as much attention as he usually pays to the butt of the neighbor's Chihuahua.

"He likes you," I say.

"He just wants to lick the soup off of me," she counters.

Huh. "You might be right." I look down into my dog's soulful eyes. "Are you hungry?"

Dumb question. Hearing the code word, Sir Ems waddles excitedly to the kitchen.

I sigh. "Can I feed him quickly and then give you the clothes?"

She nods.

We head to the kitchen together. As soon as we enter, she grins and says, "That's adorable."

I follow her gaze.

Sir Ems is doing his usual shtick—lying flat on his belly, his short legs stretched out behind him. "That's called a corgi sploot."

"Well, feed him. Quick. He looks like he's starving."

"Yeah, right. I fed him before I left."

I open a can of wet food and spoon it into a metal bowl. As Sir Ems attacks it, I lead Kendall to the closet.

"Take whatever you want. You can shower and change in there." I gesture at the bathroom.

She dubiously eyes the closet and then the bathroom.

"Don't worry," I say. "While you do that, I'll take the dog for a walk."

Is that relief on her face? It seems a little like disappointment.

"I'll ring the doorbell when we're done," I continue.

"Thank you," she says.

"Don't mention it." I head over to the kitchen, where Sir Ems is already done and looking at me with an expression that says he could go for seconds. And thirds.

"How about we take a walk?" I offer.

This keyword makes him almost as happy as the promise of food. He trots over to the shoe rack, grabs his leash, and drags it over to me, his tail wagging approaching the speed of a helicopter blade.

"All right," I say. "We'll be back soon."

I close the door and do my best not to picture Kendall stripping by my closet.

Or naked in my shower.

Or—

Fuck me.

This is going to be one very uncomfortable walk.

CHAPTER 7

Kendall

AS SOON AS THEY LEAVE, I secure myself inside the apartment with the door chain, just in case, then head over to the kitchen and grab a garbage bag along with one of those heavy-duty Ziplocs.

As I walk to the bathroom, I can't help but take in my surroundings. Between the posters of MMA fighters on the walls and the spartan furniture, the place screams "bachelor pad." Only the dog accouterments take away from that impression.

When I get to the bathroom, I smile at the lack of lotions, hair conditioners, and bath things, like salts, oils, and bombs. No woman has utilized this bathroom for any length of time—or if she has, Ash must've been ruthless at excommunicating any hint of her.

I take the soup-drenched clothes off and stash them in the garbage bag. When I get to my socks, I hide them in the Ziploc, making sure to seal in the smell, and stash them next to the bag with the gym socks. Next, I start the shower and use the handled showerhead to rinse off the parts of me that came into contact with the soup.

As I do so, I'm tempted to direct the spray at my clit until I achieve a happy ending, the way I sometimes do at home. But it doesn't feel right to do it in someone else's shower. It would be like Ash stroking his cock in my shower.

Holy shit. Why did I go there? The image makes me want to have my way with the showerhead and then go for seconds with my fingers.

No. I'm not going to abuse Ash's hospitality like that. It will have to wait until I get home.

Proud of my restraint, I step out of the shower, towel off, and put my underwear back on. Grabbing another towel, I wrap it around myself and return to the closet, where I choose a pair of new-looking sweatpants, a T-shirt with pictures of two corgis in identical positions labeled "sitting" and "standing," and a gray hoodie.

As I put it on, Ash's distinctive, yummy smell envelops me, making me wet all over again.

Damn it. I should've done the taco handshake in the shower while I had the chance. Or, according to Ash's argument that tacos are hot dogs, would it be the hot dog handshake? No… that would mean something very different.

Grr. Where is Ash? As soon as he's back, I can rush home and take care of business there, like a normal person.

The doorbell rings.

Speak of the devil.

I head over to the front door and remove the chain. "Come in."

Sir Ems enters first, dancing with excitement as if we were best friends who haven't seen each other in a few years. Ash follows, unhooking his short-legged friend from the leash and giving him a bone to chew.

"Feeling better?" He looks me over approvingly.

"Sure." If by "better," he means soup-free. As far as my libido goes, I—

"Did you decide if you want to go to a museum, see a Broadway show, or take a stroll in Central Park for our next date?"

I snort. "That wasn't as smooth as you probably thought it was."

At the same time, the idea that there will be another date does all sorts of funny things to the proverbial butterflies in my belly.

"But you're thinking about it," he says confidently.

"Am I?" I take my phone out. "Here. Put in your contact info and call your phone so we have a way to get in touch. We'll work out the details later."

He accepts my phone and does as I said. When he hands it back to me, his fingers brush mine, and my breath stills in my lungs. My eyes lock with his, and the world around us seems to fade as my skin heats and my heart thuds in a fast, uneven rhythm.

"Kendall…" His voice is low and husky as his gaze falls to my lips. He looks to be in the grip of the same madness, his golden skin tinged with color and his nostrils flaring as he stares at my mouth. "May I kiss you?"

No. No way.

At least that's what I should say. Because I've sworn off men, especially good-looking, charming ones like Ash. Because I don't need another heartbreak coming so soon on the heels of the last one. Because if he kisses me, it won't stop there, and it'll be awkward the next morning. Because—

"Yes." The word escapes my lips unbidden, and before I can take it back, he swoops in and claims his kiss.

CHAPTER 8

Ashton

HER LIPS ARE THE SOFTEST, most delicious things I've ever tasted. I want more. More of her. More of—

Lips glued to mine, she reaches for the hem of the hoodie I lent her and, pulling back for a second, yanks it off over her head. With a low growl, I drag her back in to resume the kiss, and as our lips meet, I deepen it, exploring her mouth with my tongue as she reaches for her T-shirt.

Fuck, yeah.

My heart rate triples, and my cock reaches new levels of hardness. I need her so badly I all but shake with it. Breathing raggedly, I help her get her T-shirt off as she helps me with mine, each brush of her slim, manicured fingers over my bare skin sending scorching heat through my veins.

By the time those nimble fingers reach for the

zipper of my jeans, I'm barely coherent with my need for her. I've never wanted a woman so badly, not even as a horny teen before my first fuck. Something about her taste, her feel, the way her body arches against me as her fingers fumble with my fly melts every neuron in my brain, transforming me into a pillaging barbarian. I all but devour her as our clothes drop to the floor in a trail that leads to my bedroom, and then I'm splaying her out on my bed, so overcome by lust it's all I can do to pull back for a second to take in her sleek, naked curves.

Her creamy, unblemished skin all but glows under the soft light emitted by my bedside lamp, its smoothness unreal as I run my fingers over her slender ribcage and palm her small, round breasts.

"Gorgeous." The word comes out on a low rasp as I brush my thumbs over her peaked nipples. "So. Fucking. Gorgeous."

Her gaze meets mine, her hazel eyes dark in the dim light. Her pink tongue strokes over her kiss-swollen lips, making my cock jump. "Do you… have a condom?" She darts a glance at my groin, and her eyes widen. "That is, if they make them big enough."

"Sure." My voice is hoarse. I tear my gaze away from the naked perfection of her body long enough to rummage in my nightstand and pull out a foil packet that reads "EXTRA LARGE."

My hands are not entirely steady, so I rip open the packet with my teeth before sheathing myself. She watches hungrily, her chest rising and falling in the most tantalizing manner, and as I climb over her and she reaches for me, pulling me in for another kiss, I know I'm about to lose control.

"I want you," she whispers in my ear, her breath sending goosebumps down the side of my body as her slender hand curves around my cock, guiding me to the tender opening of her body. "Ash, I—"

I slant my lips over hers, not wanting to hear the wrong name on her lips. I probably should've corrected her before now, told her I'm a substitute for the trainer she was supposed to see, but it doesn't matter now. None of it matters as the head of my cock sinks into her, and I feel how soft and wet she is. So fucking wet and tight I nearly come right then and there.

It takes everything I have not to thrust all the way in in one hard stroke. Instead, I go in slowly, letting her adjust to my size, even though the barbarian inside me howls in protest.

"Oh, fuck," she breathes against my lips, her nails digging into my shoulders as I push in deeper. "Oh, holy fuck."

Holy fuck is right. This is fucking sublime. By the time I bottom out inside her, we're both panting and sweating—and it's only the beginning. Pulling out, I slowly thrust back in as her nails dig deeper into my skin, and then... then I begin to fuck her in earnest, the barbarian unleashed.

By the time I come, she's full-on screaming, and I've

counted at least three orgasms if the squeezing of her inner muscles is anything to go by.

Spent and exhausted, I roll onto my side and gather her into my embrace, breathing in her apple and hibiscus scent mixed with the musk of sex.

It's official.

I can't wait to fucking do this again.

CHAPTER 9
Kendall

I WAKE up enveloped in strong arms.

What?

Oh, right. The X-rated events of the past evening—particularly all the toe-curling orgasms—flood my brain with NSFW images.

And holy crap. Despite the soreness that I feel from the epic encounter, I'm getting hot and bothered, again.

Oh, no. I wriggle out of the yummy arms and, careful not to jostle the bed too much, check my phone.

Shit. Tierre has sent everyone a bat emoji, followed by a police car light emoji, followed by SOS. He calls this "the bat signal," but we call it "the batshit signal" behind his back. When this text arrives, everyone who works for Tierre is expected to drop everything and report to the shoot posthaste, or seek other employment.

What kind of emergency can there be at five-twenty in the morning?

The answer comes immediately.

Tony ate Milk.

If I were alone, I'd groan. Tony is the name of the white tiger, and Milk is—was—the name of the giant albino iguana. Everyone but Tierre saw this "emergency" coming a mile away, but Tierre claimed, and I quote: "Tony is a sweetheart. He wouldn't hurt a fly. Besides, he's lactose intolerant."

Yeah. Try to argue with that level of logic. Also— and most importantly—what can I do to help in this situation? I'm not an animal trainer, nor an animal funeral director, nor a medium who speaks to the ghosts of iguanas.

Still, I don't really have a choice, so I furtively get up —because I see no reason to wake up Ash at this ungodly hour.

Yep. By sneaking out, I'm being considerate, and not cowardly… at all.

I'll write him a note saying I had to go.

No. Better. A text later today.

Collecting the clothes I borrowed, I tiptoe all the way to the front door—only to bump into Sir Ems, who wags his tail at me with too much enthusiasm considering he's not had his morning coffee yet.

"It was nice to meet you," I whisper. "You're officially my second favorite Ems in the whole wide world."

He trots over and pokes my shin with his nose.

"Yeah." I pat his head. "I'll miss you too."

With that, I sneak out, closing the door softly behind me, and rush to deal with the SOS.

When I reach the shoot, I'm tempted to rub my eyes.

Even if this were South Florida, I'd still say this is an obscene number of iguanas. There are green iguanas, brown iguanas, gray iguanas, pale yellow iguanas, eating iguanas, humping iguanas, but notably, not a single white one with pink eyes, like the late Milk, which is what Mr. Boss is screaming about.

"The noun for a collection of iguanas is a 'mess,'" Catherine whispers to me conspiratorially. "I think it's apropos to our current situation."

Yep. It's a mess. Everyone does their best not to look Tierre in the eye, except maybe the tiger, who's eyeing the mess of iguanas like an all-you-can-eat buffet.

"You!" Tierre's bejeweled finger jabs pointedly in my direction. "Is that a fashion statement?"

Shit. I'm dressed in Ash's hoodie and sweatpants. "This is what I sleep in," I say sheepishly. "When I got your text, I didn't think there was time to change."

He nods, as if what I said was in any way reasonable. "Do you have a solution?"

My throat is drier than the desert, which works out because when my heart jumps into it, it stays put in my body. "I'd use that one." I point at the palest yellow iguana in the mess. "Then you can 'pale it up' in post-production."

He wrinkles his nose.

"Or," I quickly say, "if editing photos is unthinkable, we could cover the iguana in foundation and give it some sort of vampire contacts."

Tierre's eyes light up. "We'll give him a makeover. The models too."

"There you go." I really hope he doesn't make the models look like vampiric iguanas, but he probably will —and the fashion world will eat that up just as eagerly as everything else he excretes.

"Keep this up," he says. "I knew you'd be useful if you got rid of the mopey juju, and I was right, as usual."

"Thank you." It takes a lot of effort not to put a question mark at the end of that sentence.

He approaches me—as in, advances way into my personal space—then takes my chin and twists my head left and right.

"You haven't just lost the mope," he says, and for some reason, his breath smells exactly like the citrus notes of Chanel Coco Mademoiselle. "You've done a three-sixty. You're glowing now."

If I'd done a three-sixty, I'd be back in mope land. Obviously, I don't inform Mr. Boss of this. I just mutter "thank you" instead.

"You're welcome," he says imperiously and leaves my personal space in order to shout commands at his other minions.

A slender hand lands on my shoulder. "I think it is me everyone should be thanking," Catherine murmurs.

I turn her way. "I agree, but... why this time?"

She pulls me aside. "You saw Ash, didn't you?"

I nod.

"And now you're glowing." She looks at me like "connect the dots already."

I stare at her. How could she know why I'm glowing? Does she smell sex on me, like a dog? For that matter, is that what her husband picked up on as well—my orgasms?

"I know exactly how you feel," she says. "Ash is so amazing. He left me equally speechless and glowing... countless times."

"What?" The question comes out angrier than appropriate for work.

Catherine cocks her head. "I told you: Tierre and I are in an open marriage, so you don't need to be so indignant. In fact, he likes it when I—"

"But... are you saying Ash sleeps with *all* his clients?" I hold my breath as I wait for her answer, but I already know what she's going to say.

"Not all. Just the female ones," she clarifies. "When Tierre took a session, he got an actual workout."

I feel like I've been sucker punched. In my ovaries. And then had them extracted without anesthesia.

"He's... a gigolo?"

Catherine giggles. "Don't be silly. That's such an outdated term. He's a personal trainer with benefits. Have you never heard of such a thing?"

I shake my head, and she tells me about her tennis coach, who goes down on her, and her pool boy, who's a great foot masseuse, and her plumber, who services all sorts of openings that aren't pipes.

With every word she speaks, I feel more and more nauseated.

Catherine's phone rings just as she was about to tell me what she does with her accountant. Apologizing, she picks up, and when the call is over, she says, "It's about to start. Let's go."

"What's about to start?"

A porn film where Ash is the lead? An orgy where he fucks every female that I work with?

Nothing would surprise me at this point.

"Milk's funeral," she says. "Or wake. Or repass. I'm not sure what the terminology should be, given that there's no body to bury."

Did I say nothing would surprise me? I should know better than to even think such a thing when Tierre is involved.

So, yeah, the whole crew celebrates the life and the ultimate sacrifice of Milk the Iguana, and if Tierre were to give such a genuinely heartfelt speech at *my* funeral, it would almost make getting eaten by a tiger worth it in the end.

"You've impressed me twice in one day," Tierre says to me when the service is over. "You're the only person besides myself who's truly grieving for dear Milk."

I nod solemnly, not about to tell him that I'm not. What he saw was my being upset that yet another guy turned out to be a dog. A manwhore. A clever one too, because he somehow made me feel like I was special. Like maybe the two of us might have—

"Okay, the service is over," Tierre says. "And the shoot is about to start, so…"

I channel all my acting prowess into a semi-human smile. "Don't worry. I'll be fine."

Grunting with approval, Tierre turns on his heel and flits away on a cloud of perfume.

Hey. I didn't lie. I will be fine. Eventually.

Taking out my phone, I find Ash's number, and without hesitation, I block and delete it.

There.

The path to being fine has already begun.

CHAPTER 10

Ashton

WHEN I WAKE UP, I'm alone in my bed.

Weird.

"Kendall?"

No reply.

I get up and check the bathroom.

Nope. She's missing, and so are the clothes she borrowed.

Confused, I check the kitchen just in case, but she's not there either.

Okay. It's official. She's not in the apartment.

And there's no note. No call. No text.

Very weird.

"What about you?" I say to Sir Ems. "Did you see her?"

He wags his tail, but I can't tell if that means yes or no.

I do know what his eyes are saying, though, so I

feed him, then eat some oatmeal and take him for a walk, bringing my phone with me just in case.

No luck. Even by evening, there's nothing. Does that mean last night was just a one-night stand for her? Is that why she did the Irish goodbye thing?

Screw that.

I pull out my phone and text her.

No reply comes. Not that evening, not the next morning, and not at any point in the next few days. And with each passing hour, I get more and more irrationally upset.

What the fuck? I thought we had a really good connection, and the sex was out of this fucking world.

If any other woman had done this to me—though none ever have—I would think "good riddance" and move on. But for some reason, with Kendall, I can't bring myself to do that. So I try calling her over the weekend, only to get her voicemail.

I debate hanging up—and again, with any other woman I would—but I feel compelled to say something.

"Hey, Kendall. I think I'm getting the message, but just in case you're simply not a great communicator, I want to tell you that I had a great time and would like to see you again."

There. The ball is officially in her ghostly court.

Right?

Or should I try something else?

Would I seem like a stalker if I did?

Fuck. I can't believe a woman I've known for such a

short time has me so wound up. I literally want to chase her down, throw her over my shoulder, bring her to my bedroom, and demand to know what the fuck went wrong. And after she explains—and it'd better be something good, like her grandmother died and she had to fly to a cell-phone-free resort in Timbuktu to bury her—I want to fuck her brains out and make her promise never to do this again.

Yeah, I'm officially losing it.

I think I need some perspective.

Taking my phone out, I sprawl on my couch and dial my sister, Jordan.

"Hey, bro," she says, intentionally trying to sound like a fraternity douche.

"Hey, Jojo," I say. "I need your expertise."

"Oh? And you think calling me Jojo will make me want to help you?"

I sigh. I forgot she hates her childhood nickname. "I'm sorry, *Jordan*."

"That's better. What's up?"

"I met this girl—" I start, only to be interrupted by a squeal.

"Tell me everything!"

So I tell her about the events that transpired before Kendall came to my place, ending on, "What happened next is the kind of thing where a gentleman doesn't go into detail."

"Eww. But if you got that far, what's the problem?"

"She was gone in the morning."

"Just poof and gone?" Jordan asks.

"Exactly. No note, no text, no voicemail. And she hasn't replied to any of my texts or picked up the phone when I've called."

"Huh." I swear I can hear her scratching her head on the other end. "Usually, it's the guy who does the ghosting after they get the sex, but—"

"Did some guy do that to you?" My fist clenches involuntarily.

"I was talking hypothetically," she says, a little too quickly for my liking. "But yeah. You got ghosted."

"But why?"

"Who knows? If I start to speculate, I might need to go into your performance during the icky part of the story."

"I know for a fact that's not it."

"But—and prepare to have your mind blown— women *can* fake it. Also, and I repeat, eww."

I blow out a frustrated breath. "Something must have happened. I need to get it sorted out. They have her info at the gym, so I'll just—"

"Hell, no. That's a stalker move. If you want my advice: forget her and find someone who is worthy of a guy as awesome as you."

I force myself to ignore the peculiar tightness in my chest. "Maybe you're right." I shouldn't let a girl I only spent one night with have this kind of hold over me. "Anyway, how are things with you?"

"Oh, same old. Spoke to Dad the other day and Mom the day prior, so there's *that*."

"Which was it: a guilt trip or 'I'm disappointed in you?'"

"A little bit of both," she says. "When did you speak to them last?"

"Their birthdays."

"Lucky. Anything else up with you, besides the Kendall fiasco?"

"Nope, just like you said. Same old."

"In that case, I'd better run," she says. "Oh, and I must add: You've gotten wiser over the years."

"How so?"

"You thought to call me."

With that, she hangs up.

I wait a beat, battling the heavy feeling in my chest. Then I open my contacts, locate Kendall's number, and delete it.

Jordan is right. It's over.

I doubt I'll ever see Kendall again.

PART TWO

Present Day

CHAPTER 11

Kendall

"YES, TIERRE," I say into my phone. "I told the dry-cleaning lady that her service was 'merde.'" And then thanked my lucky stars she didn't know French.

I suppress a sigh. Ever since Mr. Boss sniffed out that I want to be a designer myself, he's dangled opportunities in front of me, but of course, said opportunities have come at a cost: I'm even more like an indentured servant these days.

"And you found a replacement?" he demands.

I don't bother reminding him that today is Saturday, which means I'm supposed to only be available to him for emergencies. "I found replacements, plural. A new dry-cleaning place, friendlier landscapers, and an aesthetician who says she can wax anything you want and at any time of day." Except Sunday mornings, but that's okay because that's the time Tierre usually sleeps in.

"Keep it up," Mr. Boss says and hangs up.

Whew. I was afraid Tierre would get wind of the fact that I'm about to have brunch at a restaurant that even he can't get into willy-nilly.

I still can't believe *I'm* going to have brunch here, among all the models and celebs. And billionaires, like Emma's new boyfriend, Marcus Carelli.

Yeah, that's a new development, and an unexpected one. I mean, the dude is a Wall Street whizz who's graced the cover of *Forbes* more than once—and my cat lady friend is dating him. Not that Emma isn't gorgeous. Underneath her frumpy clothes, she's totally hot, with her wild red hair and J. Lo. booty, but she's barely dated anyone in the past couple of years. And then to score a billionaire?

I'm genuinely impressed, and more than a little jealous.

"Do you have a reservation?" the hostess—who totally did a few photoshoots for us a few months back—demands as I step in.

"Yes. It's under Carelli."

Her eyes widen. "Oh. I see. Right this way." She leads me to a table in the back, and as I walk through the restaurant, I spot two female reality TV stars, a lead from the latest Marvel movie, and the male model who has a restraining order against Tierre.

I'm so excited I might pee my pants.

Almost as soon as I take a seat, Emma walks in with her billionaire.

My jaw falls open.

Firstly, Marcus is infinitely more handsome and

intimidating in person. I can see why he's swept Emma off her feet even though she claims he's not her type. With his dark, boldly masculine features, powerful build, and piercing blue eyes, I'm pretty sure he's everyone's type. And would be even if he weren't a freaking billionaire.

Secondly, and more importantly, Emma has had a makeover! Her worn-out, cat-hair-covered clothes and Walmart shoes are nowhere in sight. Instead, she's wearing a hipster-cool dress-and-booties combo, and her long, bouncy red curls frame her face in a stylish new manner.

"Ems!" I yell as they approach the table. "Wow, look at your dress! And your hair! What did you do and when?"

And why was I not involved? I'm the friend who's in fashion, after all, so if—

"Got a haircut at a new place yesterday and did a little shopping," she says, beaming at me. "You like?"

"I love it!" And I do. I love the new look, and I love the way she looks next to her very rich, very male accessory.

I give my bestie a hug, then turn to Marcus. "Doesn't she look absolutely stunning?"

His gaze travels hungrily over Emma. "Yes. Always."

Oh, wow. I barely resist the urge to fan myself. The two of them in real life is what porn would look like if it were made by Hallmark. The chemistry is palpable. His eyes say that he'd gladly fuck her right here and now, and it would be a no-holds-barred fuck.

Do I sound pervy? I think I do. It must be my viciously long dry spell talking.

Clearing my throat, I thrust out my hand at Emma's boyfriend. "Kendall Bryce. I don't think we've ever formally introduced ourselves." '

"Marcus Carelli," he replies. "It's nice to formally meet you, Kendall."

"Marcus's friend, Ashton, is joining us for lunch," Emma tells me as we sit down and the waiter brings a pitcher of water for the table. "I told Marcus you wouldn't mind."

A friend? Another billionaire, hopefully. "Of course not. The more, the merrier." I wait until Marcus looks down at the menu, then catch Emma's gaze and pantomime swooning.

Emma's lips twitch like she's about to laugh, but then she looks at her boyfriend and I suddenly feel like a third wheel.

"So, Marcus," I say when he raises his eyes from the menu. "Emma told me the two of you are doing a trial run of living together. How is that going so far? Are you surviving the feline invasion?"

He grins. "For the most part. I did wake up the other morning with a furry butt on my face, but Emma assured me that the cats clean themselves thoroughly—and that Mr. Puffs didn't sneak into the bedroom and try to smother me on purpose."

"Oh, no," I say with a laugh. "I'd be careful if I were you. The things I've heard about that cat…"

"All true," Marcus says. "He may indeed be of

demonic origin. Luckily, his siblings are quite harmless, and I largely get along with them."

"He's being modest," Emma says, laying a hand on his sleeve. "Cottonball has fallen head over heels in love with him. He follows Marcus around like a puppy."

Before I can reply, the waiter comes over to take our drink orders. Emma—being her usual frugal, pathologically independent self—asks for plain water, while I get a hibiscus iced tea and so does Marcus.

Just as the waiter leaves, a man approaches our table, and I automatically scan him, starting with his shoes.

He's wearing Italian loafers. Armani jeans. A light-colored cashmere sweater that he fills out very nicely. I can tell his face will be attractive even before I lift my gaze.

Oh. Fuck.

I know this face.

This is—

"Great call on the place," the newcomer says to Marcus as he takes a seat next to me. "I've been meaning to try it, but you beat me to it."

What. The. Actual. Fuck.

The last time I saw him, he was—

"Ashton Vancroft," he says to me with a smile that is as fake as it is wide. "And you are?"

To add insult to injury, he extends his hand to me.

I give him my most withering glare.

"Kendall Bryce," I grit out.

He keeps his fucking hand out, which makes me

want to stab it with the butter knife. But I'm not the kind of person who makes a scene, so with great effort, I ignore the proffered appendage and angle my chair so I don't have to look at his smug, gorgeous face.

Shit.

Maybe I have made a scene, after all.

Emma is gaping at me.

This is just great. I never told her about my one-night stand with this literal manwhore, so—

"So," Ash—or Ashton, or whatever the fuck his full name is—drawls. "What's good here?"

Looking puzzled, Emma's boyfriend says wryly, "Everything, I assume." Then he cocks an eyebrow. "Do you two know each other?"

"No." I flag down our waiter and, when he hurries over, order a pitcher of sangria.

This is what I get for not telling my best friend about the hottest—and most humiliating—one-night stand of my life.

"Are you going to share that?" Ashton—as I've decided to call him in an effort not to think about that night—asks, his eyes gleaming with amusement. "Or are you planning to drink the whole thing by yourself?"

My fists itch. Would it be considered a scene if I punched his fucking face as my reply?

Emma clears her throat. "So, Ashton, how is your business going? Any luck slowing down that revenue growth?"

Business? Revenue growth? Just how many women has he been "training?" Must be a lot, judging by those nice clothes he's wearing. He totally looks like he belongs here, with the rich and famous. There's even a subtle air of commanding arrogance around him, the same kind of power that Marcus Carelli exudes.

Except Marcus is a genuine self-made billionaire, and his friend is a "personal trainer with benefits." How do the two of them even know each other?

Then again, Carelli wasn't always a billionaire. In fact, he's a classic rags-to-riches story, so this could be a friend from his rags days. Except Emma's boyfriend went into finance, while his friend decided to fuck his way into money.

Damn it. Now I have a mental image of his massive cock poking through a hundred-dollar bill. A weirdly hot, unwelcome image that—

"Afraid not," the asshole replies with a grimace. "It's like a snowball rolling down a mountain—just keeps gathering momentum."

Now I see an image of a snowball covered with dicks. Wait, why multiple dicks? Or any?

As I'm trying to untangle that puzzle, Ashton looks from Emma to Marcus. "How about you two lovebirds? How's everything? Is the wedding date already set?"

Emma bursts out laughing. "Oh, yes. It's tomorrow night at Disney World. Six o'clock. Be there or meet Mickey's wrath."

She's referring to a gossip rag article about the two of them with the clickbait headline of "Is One of New York's Most Eligible Getting Hitched at Disney World?"

Yes, that's right. My best friend now shows up in gossip rags. Like a freaking celebrity.

Marcus doesn't look amused. Instead, he eyes Ashton like he'd help me punch his friend in the balls... for starters.

Ashton must feel our joint wrath because he clears his throat and motions to the waiter, who comes over with the same record-setting speed.

"What have you got on tap?" Ashton asks, and the waiter rattles off a list of beer names.

Ashton orders one, and Marcus gets one too—which means that the pitcher of sangria is going to just be for me, after all. Which is fine.

I'm pretty sure I'll need it.

"So, everyone," Marcus says. "What are your Christmas plans?"

I do my best to pull myself together and tell them I'll be seeing my family. My nemesis says he has the same plans, though he doesn't sound terribly excited. I wonder if it's because his parents disapprove of his chosen profession.

If so, I don't blame them.

Picking up on the continuing tension, Marcus steers the conversation back to Emma's cats and their shenanigans—which, annoyingly, makes me remember Ashton's dog, Sir Ems. Still, I laugh at the cat stories, if only halfheartedly, and avoid looking at Ashton because that way lies causing a worse scene.

When the appetizers arrive, I excuse myself to go to the bathroom. Emma is waiting for me when I emerge from the stall, but I avoid her gaze, not ready to answer her inevitable questions.

I don't know why I haven't told her what happened three years ago, but I'm even less inclined to do so now.

When I get back to the table, Marcus and Emma do their best to make the meal less awkward, but what it actually takes is three glasses of sangria, after which the buzz takes some of the edge off and allows me to tell them about the crazy errands Tierre sends me on.

"Why?" Emma asks when I describe the time Mr. Boss tasked me with locating him a female virgin with his exact blood type.

I shrug. "He read that giving an older person a blood transfusion from a younger person can make the former feel more youthful."

"I think the 'why' Emma meant was, 'Why a virgin?'" Marcus chimes in.

"My boss's mind works in mysterious ways?"

To prove this point, I tell them a few more anecdotes in the same vein, but then the conversation veers toward crazy dating stories, so I share about the guy who was dead set on showing me his ex-girlfriend's picture, no matter what I said. As I go on, I notice Ashton squeezing his fork and glaring at me through a clenched-teeth smile.

Huh.

Is he afraid I'll tell them the story of how we met?

Serves him right, but no. That isn't what I want either, so we end up talking about our favorite shows and movies instead—because that's safe... unless someone here is an avid fan of *Deuce Bigalow: Male Gigolo*.

The conversation flows, and I manage not to cause a scene until the check comes, which is when Marcus and Ashton start fighting over who'll pay it—and decide to split it in half. As if I were Ashton's date.

Oh, no. Fuck that.

Normally, I don't mind letting a guy pay for me, but not Ashton.

Never Ashton.

Unable to stop myself from shooting Ashton another glare, I whip out my credit card and plunk it into the waiter's hand, telling him to put my portion of the bill on it.

"This isn't a double date," I say to Emma when she raises her freshly groomed eyebrows.

Without waiting for a reply, I chug the rest of my sangria, and as soon as the waiter comes back, I sign the check, mumble a rushed farewell to Emma and Marcus, and hurry out as fast as my Manolo Blahniks can carry me.

THE FIRST THING I DO WHEN I GET HOME IS PACK MY shoes in a plastic bag and seal it thoroughly to lock in the odor. The second thing I do is brainstorm something I should've figured out as soon as I finished my MFA: a dress design that is completely my own. That lasts about thirty seconds before I give in to temptation and look up Ashton Vancroft.

Holy fuck.

He's got a whole fitness empire now. His ThriveFit app is at the top of all the app stores' charts, with ravingly great reviews, and his clients include every celebrity I can think of.

And there are interviews with the asshole. Tons of them.

How did I manage to miss his rapid ascent? Normally, I know everyone and everything.

The only explanation I can think of is that after that night, I've pathologically avoided anything to do with gyms and fitness, my morning runs excluded.

In a moment of weakness, I click on a video of an interview with him and hear in his own words how the techie side of his business began when he wanted to help his clients remotely but couldn't find an app that did everything he needed—so he had one created.

Stopping the video, I snort.

Help his clients remotely. What is that a euphemism for—phone sex or sexting?

Resuming the video, I listen to the rest and cringe as Ashton pretends that he cares nothing about the financial aspect of his achievements.

"Ultimately, I'm in the business of bringing happiness," he says. "And that's all I care about."

Somehow, that just makes me angrier—because in a fucked-up way, it's probably true. "Bringing happiness" one orgasm at a time was what he was doing when I met him. Catherine sure seemed happy with his services.

Maybe I should've been too?

No, fuck that. I didn't know he was simply rendering services. He made me feel special, like what happened between us was unique—until I learned there was a conveyor belt of other women who felt exactly the same.

Well, whatever. Clearly, his strategy worked, and he's insanely rich now. If not a billionaire like Marcus, then well on his way. No wonder he was dressed so nicely at that brunch—it's all chump change to him now.

I must be a masochist because I pull up more articles about him and learn that he actually comes from old money. Which explains his air of commanding arrogance. Come to think of it, he even had it when we met three years ago, when he was still just a trainer who was working through the *Kama Sutra* with his clients on the side.

Ugh. I need to stop thinking about him. Delete him from my mind the way I did from my phone.

So that's exactly what I try to do for the next few days: I refuse to talk about him no matter how hard Emma pries. I even manage to resist Emma's most enhanced interrogation technique—a shopping trip for Manolo Blahniks.

CHAPTER 12

Ashton

MARCUS and I are covered in sweat as we circle each other in the octagon.

Today is different from our usual in that Marcus seems to want to cause real damage to me. The only reason he doesn't succeed is because we've been sparring together for years, and I know all his moves.

"Listen," I say as I dodge a lightning-fast jab. "Is this about my stupid joke about the wedding?"

His reply is a low kick, which I dodge.

"I didn't mean to put you in an awkward position." Or if I did, only a little.

He swings at me again.

Fuck this. My next argument is a roundhouse kick.

And so it goes, until Marcus's phone timer informs us that the session is over.

"So… we good?" I ask as we regain our breath in the locker room.

"Fine," he says through clenched teeth. "Just watch what you say around Emma in the future."

"Deal."

The truth is, I plan to avoid Emma as much as I can because where she goes, Kendall might follow. Then again, why should I avoid my friend's woman just because—

"Now that that's cleared up," Marcus says, "I'm obligated to ask: how do you know Kendall?"

Fuck. Did he just read my mind or something? "Emma didn't tell you?"

And if she did, what did she say? That her friend had a one-night stand with me?

"No."

I frown. "Don't girls share shit like that?"

He shrugs. "Apparently, Emma has been pestering Kendall for over a week and hasn't gotten any results. So whatever happened, it must've been very private."

I give him a level stare. "I will neither confirm nor deny that."

"Seriously?"

I shrug. "A gentleman doesn't kiss and tell."

"A *gentleman* doesn't. What does that have to do with you?"

I slam the locker door. "This conversation is over."

"Fair enough. You'll tell me when you're good and ready."

It will be a freezing day in hell when I do. "Since you brought her up, what do *you* know about Kendall?" I ask, and at his smug expression, I regret it instantly.

"Her family must be wealthy, or so I assume because Emma told me her parents pay most of Kendall's bills," he answers, smirking. "She's a good friend to Emma. Does something in fashion. If you want to know more, I have a guy."

He must mean the guy who put together a dossier on Emma for him. "No, thanks." Since I know Kendall's last name now, I can poke around on social media myself. And it won't be a stalker move. At all.

"You'd make a great couple," Marcus says with a bigger smirk. "Isn't that what's most important?"

"Fuck you." I stride out of the locker room.

As I ride home in an Uber, I replay the cursed brunch in my head once again.

When I walked in, I couldn't believe my eyes. I've thought about Kendall often over the past three years, especially if you stretch the definition of the word "thought" to include "jerked off to." And I've regretted listening to my sister and not looking up Kendall's info at the gym right away. Three months after our one-night stand, in a moment of weakness, I caved and went to Essence to ask Gerald for her file—only to learn that the gym's computers recently got a virus that wiped out nearly all of their data, client records included.

It was the most intense disappointment I'd ever felt, second only to discovering her gone that morning.

I told myself it was a sign that I needed to let go and forget her, to focus on other things. And I tried my hardest to do so, throwing myself wholeheartedly into my work, with the result that my business has taken off beyond my wildest dreams.

It's possible that a part of me secretly hoped she'd come across my app or catch a glimpse of one of my media appearances and regret walking away from what we could've had.

And then there she was, sitting at the table with Marcus and his girlfriend, looking stylish as fuck and so beautiful it set my teeth on edge... and had other, more X-rated effects on one specific part of my body. The temptation to march over there and throw her over my shoulder so I could carry her off and demand answers—after first fucking her brains out, of course—was so strong I all but shook with it.

It took everything I had to walk over as if she meant nothing—and then to pretend like we've never met before. Because it was either that or cause a major scene.

As a bonus, acting the way I did seemed to piss her off.

Why did it piss her off, by the way? It was almost like—

No. There's no figuring out her mind. If there were, I would know why she ghosted me three years ago. Not that I haven't developed a theory: it's because she's too fancy to date a lowly personal trainer, which is what I was back then.

I wonder what she thinks of me now that I'm wealthy and successful.

No. There's no point in wondering. It doesn't

matter. If wealth and status are all she cares about, goodbye and good riddance. And if I've looked her up on social media a few times—okay, more than a few times—over the past week, it's purely out of curiosity, nothing else.

My phone rings.

I check the screen and sigh. It's Jordan, but she's calling from her work number, meaning she's about to talk to me as my CTO.

"Hey, sis," I say, picking up.

"Don't call me 'sis' when I call from this number. This could've been a conference call."

"Sorry, *Jordan*. What's up?"

"There's a problem. The datacenter in—"

"Let me stop you right there. You're my top technical person, so you decide what to do."

"But we have three choices. We can either—"

"Have you made a wrong choice yet?"

"No," she says sullenly.

"Well, then, there you go."

Jordan has definitely contributed to my aforementioned wealth. Despite that, she still doesn't have enough confidence in her decision-making ability.

"Fine," she says with a sigh. "But don't you dare question my decision if it ends up costing you a fortune."

"I doubt I'll be so lucky."

She scoffs. "I'm not going to dignify that with a reply."

"Your call."

"So," she says, switching to her casual sisterly tone. "Have you seen Kendall again?"

"No, and I won't."

Speaking of bad decisions, mine was telling Jordan about the cursed brunch.

"Yes, you will," she says. "Your best friend and her best friend are getting serious. It's only a matter of time before you bump into each other again."

Fuck. I've been trying not to think about that nearly as hard as I've been fighting the urge to look her up.

At my silence, Jordan chuckles and says, "You know I'm right. Anyway, I have to run and deal with the datacenter issue that you don't want to hear about."

"Okay." I hang up and blankly stare at the passing streets.

Meeting Kendall again.

It's going to happen, no matter what I do.

And I can't say I'm not looking forward to it.

CHAPTER 13

Kendall

"A DESTINATION WEDDING?" I ask with a huge grin.

"Don't get too excited." Emma sets down her plain water on the table. "It's in Florida, not on the French Riviera or some such."

"Oh." I wasn't even thinking about the location, but given Marcus's wealth, the French Riviera makes a lot more sense than America's basement... unless you factor in Emma's grandparents who live in Florida, of course. "When?"

"Very soon," she says. "Sorry for the short notice, but—"

"Oh, don't worry about it. I'll be there."

"Great," Emma says. "Now there's this one other thing…"

The waiter comes with our food, so she stops talking for a moment.

"Yes?" I say when we're alone again.

She keeps her nose in her plate, which I find suspicious. "It will be just our closest friends and family at the wedding."

"Right… and?"

"Marcus's closest friend is Ashton," she says, finally meeting my gaze. "So obviously, he'll be there."

I nearly choke on the too-big piece of Eggs Benedict that I managed to stuff into my mouth. "At the ceremony?"

"And on the plane," she says.

"I see." I chew the egg that suddenly tastes like rubber. "I take it Marcus has had a similar talk with Ashton?"

"Ashton wasn't the one acting weird at brunch," Emma says gently. "But yes, he told him not to antagonize you."

If he's going to be breathing at the ceremony, he's going to antagonize me, but I'm not going to say that.

"Look, Ems," I say. "I will not ruin your big day. And if you don't like my behavior at the rehearsal, you can always—"

Emma snorts. "We're not having a rehearsal."

No rehearsal? Come to think of it, they didn't have an engagement party either—which spared me another encounter with Ashton.

"What about a bachelorette party?" I ask.

Emma grins. "If I were to have one, Ashton wouldn't be there anyway."

"So you're not?"

She shakes her head. "We just want to get married. Quick and easy. No fuss."

"Okay. How mad would you be if I flew separately?"

Emma's eyes widen. "You hate his company so much you'd forgo flying private?"

I shrug. "Tierre flies private all the time."

She grins again. "Doesn't he make you give him a manicure during the flight?"

"Not a manicure. I just file his nails," I say defensively.

"Yeah. That makes it less demeaning."

"It's not always me." But very often me. "If you want demeaning, he makes the new girl dance whenever we hit turbulence—and she has to incorporate each bump into the performance."

Emma rolls her eyes. "When are you going to strike out on your own?"

"Soon." In fact, escaping Tierre's clutches for good was my New Year's resolution this year, but I just haven't been able to get focused and work on my own designs—which is kind of important if you want to become a designer.

"Anyway," Emma says, realizing she's touched on a sensitive topic. "To answer your question: no. I don't mind if you *don't* fly with us."

It's my turn to grin. "You're probably going to be snuggling your husband-to-be the whole time anyway."

As usual in this type of situation, Emma's cheeks become the color of her hair.

"FLORIDUH?" TIERRE TRIES TO WRINKLE HIS NOSE, BUT IT is still too swollen from his most recent rhinoplasty. "Must you?"

"It's for my best friend's wedding." And I have unused vacation days, so this shouldn't even be a debate.

"Why can't she have the wedding in Paris?" he asks.

"I have no idea."

He sighs theatrically. "When is it then?"

I tell him.

"But… that's when Fifi needs to be taken to the vet."

Fifi is his pet chameleon who sees a reptile expert that I like to call He Who Must Not Be Named. "Have the intern take her."

"Fifi doesn't like that mopey bitch," Mr. Boss says with a straight face. "She's used to you taking her."

I set my jaw and meet his gaze. "I can't miss this wedding."

If that means he fires me, so be it. It's not like I have much more to learn from Tierre as far as designing goes, and my pay has never gotten to the point where it could cover more than my food and utility bills.

"Fine," Tierre says magnanimously. "You may go to Florida. But if you get eaten by a shark, don't come crying to me."

CHAPTER 14

Kendall

ON MY DISTINCTLY NON-PRIVATE flight to Florida, I sit in the middle seat between a woman with a screaming baby and a guy who must be allergic to soap.

I blame Ashton for this misery. If it weren't for him, I'd be on a private plane. The gentlemanly thing to do would've been for *him* to refuse to fly private, not the other way around.

"Good morning, ladies and gentlemen. This is your flight attendant speaking. Boarding is now complete."

Yep. It's officially too late to escape. Maybe I can hold my breath for the duration while plugging my ears?

My phone rings.

"Hey, Ems!" I exclaim after gladly fishing it out of my bag. "What's up? They're about to ask us to turn off our phones."

For whatever reason, the baby stops crying long enough to give me a dirty look.

"Oh, you've boarded," Emma says. "I was hoping I'd catch you before you passed security."

"Why?"

"As it turns out, Ashton is not going with us, so if you want to join us, you can."

Crap. "It's too late. They won't let me off now."

"Oh," Emma says. "Well, that sucks."

I blow out a frustrated breath. "If I'd known sooner—"

"I just found out," she says. "Apparently, Ashton just told Marcus today."

"What an asshole."

"Actually, Marcus thinks Ashton bailed for your sake."

"Yeah, right." That would make him a gentleman, but I doubt he knows the definition of the word.

Unless… he wants to avoid *me*. Which would be extra assholey of him.

"Well, I have to run," Emma says. "See you later."

"Yeah. Looking forward to it."

I hang up and take the next few breaths through my mouth—a bad idea because now instead of smelling my neighbor, I'm tasting him.

Miserable, I sit and watch the clouds cover the disappearing ground beneath us as the plane takes off.

As soon as the captain turns off the safety belt warning, the stinky guy leaps to his feet and heads to the bathroom—where he'll hopefully wash some part of his body for the first time this year.

I get up to stretch my legs and decide to use the bathroom as well. All the ones in economy class are occupied, so I confidently walk—a.k.a. sneak—into the first-class section of the plane.

Confidence is key here, and designer clothes help as well. Nobody stops me as I walk past the first-class passengers. That is, until a deep, impossibly familiar male voice says, "You've got to be fucking kidding me."

I freeze and whip my head to the left. I'm hoping I'm mistaken, but I'm not.

A pair of blue-gray eyes stares at me out of an annoyingly handsome face.

It's Mr. Manwhore himself, sitting with an open laptop on the table in front of him.

What the fuck is he doing here? And how did I not see him first?

"You're here?" I manage through clenched teeth.

His expression is just as displeased. "Clearly," he says, and now that I know that it's there, I can totally see the old money upbringing as he narrows his eyes at me. "And I could have been on Marcus's plane, which has a pool table."

I put my hands on my hips. "So it's true. You tried to avoid me?"

"It's not all about you. I didn't go because that seemed like the easiest way to avoid you spoiling the upcoming nuptials."

"Me?"

If I were Superman, I'd totally be shooting lasers from my eyes right now.

"Remember the cringy brunch?" he says. "And just look how you're acting right now."

I have to remind myself that violence is wrong. "I can obviously pretend not to hate you for a few hours."

"Hate?" He arches an arrogant eyebrow. "What did I do to you to warrant such strong feelings?"

I roll my eyes. "That's just a figure of speech. I don't know—or care enough—about you to actually hate you. I just despise your type."

He bangs his laptop shut. "What, exactly, is my type?"

"A pretty fuck boy who's spoiled by women always falling at his feet. And who's not used to someone seeing through his fake-charm act."

His slow clap is drowning in sarcasm. "Judgey much?"

Me, judgey? "Are you saying you didn't sleep with half of Manhattan?"

My voice rises, and I realize the other passengers are staring at us open-mouthed.

He narrows his eyes. "Unlike you, I don't have one-night stands."

I'm so shocked by the blatant lie that I take a step back—and smash right into a flight attendant. After mumbling my apologies, I turn back to him. "Are you actually serious right now?"

"Madam, please take a seat."

I whirl on her. "Madam? Me? Do I look like I run a brothel?"

Ashton chuckles, damn him.

The flight attendant stiffens. "If you don't take a seat, I'll have to get the Air Marshal."

"Fine. I'm going." I turn back to glare at Ashton one more time. "I hope you can at least act cordially at the wedding."

"Pot," he says with an infuriating smile. "Meet kettle."

Worried I'll get cuffed by the Air Marshal if I speak —or more precisely, scream—my mind, I stomp away and wedge myself into my middle seat.

At that moment, the baby who had finally fallen quiet resumes crying with renewed vigor. My stinky neighbor returns to his seat, and in addition to his prior stench, he now also smells like the blue liquid in plane toilets.

Oh, and speaking of toilets, I never got the chance to use one, and now it would be way too awkward to go again.

Fuming, I suffer for what feels like a hundred hours until we land. As soon as my malodorous neighbor gets up, I squeeze past him and tug on the handle of my carry-on, which appears to be stuck between two other suitcases.

Suddenly, a long, muscular arm reaches past me and carefully extricates my luggage.

My brain gives my mouth the command to say thanks, but then I see that the helper is Ashton, which might be why what escapes my lips is, "Thank fuck you."

"I'll pass," he says, holding my (quite heavy for its size) suitcase in the air, like it weighs nothing. "If I accept that 'thank you' fuck, you'll disappear without a trace again—and Emma wants you at her wedding."

I jerk my suitcase away from him, and it nearly lands on my foot. "Don't touch my things ever again."

Grunting in frustration, he turns on his heel and pushes through the people nearby back toward the front of the plane.

That's better.

I get off the plane, finally use a bathroom, and then summon an Uber. According to the app, my ride is right next to the airport and therefore five minutes away.

When I get to the curb, a passing-by limo stops in front of me, and one of the blacked-out windows rolls down, revealing Ashton. "You want a lift?"

I adore limo rides, but not at the cost of his company, so I shake my head.

"We could just sit in silence," he says. "Or discuss how we're going to make sure we don't spoil the wedding."

"The strategy is simple: don't get in my way," I snap. "As to the ride, no thanks—I've got my own car on the way."

His jaw ticks. "Come on. Get in."

"No."

He sighs. "You seriously would rather ride with a stranger? Alone?"

"Abso-fucking-lutely."

"Fucking fine then." He rolls the window back up as the limo pulls away.

Five minutes later, the limo returns, apparently having made a circle around the terminal, and the window rolls down again.

"Get in," Ashton says curtly. "Come on. Stop being so stubborn."

I glare at him. "My car is less than a minute away. The only way I'm going with you is if you strongarm me into that limo—and believe me, I will scream my head off if you try."

He rolls his eyes. "Suit yourself."

The limo pulls away again, hopefully gone for good.

Thirty seconds later, my ride shows up—a pick-up truck decorated with a sticker that proudly states: "Driver Carries No Cash, Only Ammo."

I get inside, and I guess the driver wants to stay consistent with his sticker because as I buckle in, he loads a giant handgun and tosses it into his glove compartment.

"Don't worry," he tells me. "That's Betty. She's here to protect us."

Uh-huh. I feel super safe. Also, I'd better give him a five-star review, just in case I ever happen to run into him and Betty again.

"You motherfucking fucker!" the driver roars when a

Tesla Y cuts us off—and I can see his hand twitch toward the glove compartment. Luckily, he thinks better of that impulse, instead finishing with, "I hope your wife loses the microscope that she needs to find your dick!"

No comment. Nor do I comment when a minivan in front of us makes a sudden turn without signaling. The curses my driver showers him with are even more creative, and once again, he almost reaches for Betty.

Taking my phone out, I put in the search bar: "If a cab driver shoots someone, does that make the passenger an accessory to the crime?"

Turns out, the answer is no. Not unless I were to assist him. Good. I keep that thought front and center as we narrowly avoid several more potentially deadly altercations before arriving at our destination: a mansion at a gated beachside community.

"Thanks," I say to the driver, sounding as convincing as I do when I thank Tierre for critiquing something about my outfit.

The guy grunts something unintelligible and gets my suitcase from the trunk.

To my relief, Betty stays in the glove compartment.

CHAPTER 15

Ashton

I'M STILL FUMING as I enter the mansion Marcus rented and pick a room. Why did Kendall refuse my help with her luggage and the ride I offered her... twice? What the fuck did she think I was going to do to her in the limo?

It's not like I offered her a ride on my dick.

Which, to my dick, sounds like a great idea even now that I know she hates me. For no reason whatsoever, other than some bullshit about "my type."

The mere thought of it sets my teeth on edge.

Fuck. I need to stop thinking about her before I do something I regret, like spoiling Marcus's wedding by confronting her about why she ghosted me after that night—and why she's acting like I'm the one who ghosted her.

I dump my bags on the floor and call Randy, the guy I hired to dog-sit Sir Ems.

And yes, I still fucking call him Sir Ems because the

name fits so well. Even though the name started off as a joke between me and the person I'm trying not to think about.

Randy gives me a quick update before pointing his phone's camera at my dog, who recognizes either my face on the screen or my voice. His tail is wagging incessantly.

"Do you have any questions?" I ask.

"Are you talking to me?" Randy points the camera his way.

"No, I'm waiting for Sir Ems to bark them out. Yes, you."

"In that case, no questions. I'm all set. Enjoy your vacation."

"Thanks. Let me see him again."

He does as I ask, and I tell Sir Ems that I'll be back in four days, counting today. "One for the trip, one for the wedding, one to explore something nearby, and one to fly back."

Sir Ems wags his tail approvingly, which hopefully means he's mastered counting and won't miss me too much.

"Okay. Bye, Randy. Take good care of him."

I hang up and head over to the balcony to savor some ocean air. Unfortunately, Kendall is still on my brain. And on what passes for my dick's brain.

I grit my teeth and take a seat on the lounge chair to videocall my sister.

"Hey." She's grinning as she picks up the call. "How was the flight?"

"Crazy." I set my phone on the small table. "In trying to avoid Kendall, guess who I ran into?"

"No way. She was on the plane?"

"You know it."

Jordan shakes her head. "Remind me why you tried to avoid her in the first place?"

Because I couldn't be sure of my self-control around her. "She was so prickly at the brunch, I figured she'd be just as belligerent on the flight," I say. "And since this is my best friend's wedding, I didn't want to be part of any drama. I was right too. On the plane, she told me she *hates* me."

Jordan frowns. "She does? Why?"

"Apparently, she hates my 'type.'" Which bothers me more than I'd like to admit.

Jordan's frown deepens. "What type is that? Blond? Athletic? Awesome brother?"

I almost smile at that last one. "I think she's decided I'm a player or something."

"Which you are."

"Was. Back in college. But isn't every guy?"

"Depends. I wonder why she decided that. And why did she hook up with you three years ago if that was what she thought?"

A muscle ticks in my jaw. "I've got no clue."

"Curious." Jordan scratches her chin with two fingers.

"It was probably a one-night-stand situation for her from the start," I say. "Maybe she thinks that's something my 'type' is good for—if you have the itch."

"Eww. But yeah, that's possible. Or maybe someone hurt her recently, some guy who turned out to be a player."

"You think?" The mere possibility makes me want to break the motherfucker's dick. And crush his balls.

"Yeah." Jordan's eyes shine. "And if I'm right, the solution is simple: just tell her you're not that type."

"Right. I'm sure she'll believe me."

Jordan wrinkles her nose. "Yeah, I guess that type would say they're not that type."

I narrow my eyes at her. "What would you know about that type?"

"Oh. Nothing." She bats her eyelashes innocently. "Nothing. At. All... Brother."

My phone dings.

"Speak of the she-devil," I say. "Marcus put me down as the contact for the guard at the gate, and I was just notified that one Kendall Bryce has entered the property."

"Ah," Jordan says. "In that case, you might want to put on a fresh shirt."

With that, she hangs up.

Gritting my teeth, I head back to the room, unlock my suitcase, and change into a fresh shirt—but not because Jordan said anything, and certainly not for Kendall.

I just want to feel fresh and restored.

And if I happen to look better when I run into a certain brunette—say, when I help her get her bag up the stairs because I'm a fucking gentleman—so be it.

CHAPTER 16
Kendall

WHEN BETTY and the driver depart, I roll my suitcase to the front staircase of the mansion and take it all in: the giant columns, the twenty-foot ceilings, and—thanks to it being beachfront—the smell of the salty air.

"Let me help you with that," says a deep, smooth, and all-too-familiar voice.

I narrow my eyes at Ashton, who's just exited the front doors and is coming down the stairs. "You're also staying here?"

Is it my imagination, or does he look even hotter than he did on the plane?

"Everyone is." He stops next to me and grabs my bag before I can stop him. "I thought you knew that."

I glare up at him. "If you're here, then I'm not."

Ignoring my statement, he carries my bag up the stairs with ridiculous ease. "I thought we agreed to be civil."

I hurry after him and grab the handle of my suitcase as soon as he puts it down. "And I will be. At the wedding. Tomorrow."

He blows out a frustrated breath as I begin rolling my suitcase back toward the stairs. "You can take the room that's farthest from mine."

Before I can respond, Janie—the third musketeer to me and Emma back in college—runs out and lays it on very thick about how happy she is to see me.

Fuck. I can't bail now. Ever since Janie started dating her current boyfriend, whom I've dubbed Mr. Suck-Up, two things have drastically changed: her appearance and how frequently we hang out. If I walk away without explaining my beef with Ashton, she'll think it a snub to her.

So I pointedly ignore Ashton's glare as I wheel my suitcase deeper into the mansion, with Janie trotting next to me and telling me all about how she and her boyfriend flew on Marcus's plane, along with everyone else—and had a blast, of course.

"One second," I tell Janie, stopping as I realize I don't know where I'm going. Pasting on a fake smile, I turn around to face Ashton, who's standing in the entryway, watching us with slitted eyes. "Which room should I take?"

As in, which is the farthest from his?

He gestures at the south wing. "Third door on the left. Help yourself."

And before I can reply, he disappears down the hallway opposite the entryway.

"What was that about?" Janie asks. "Do you know him?"

"No." If I didn't explain this to Emma, I'm certainly not going to share with Janie.

"Well, I think he likes you," she says. "He was eyeing you like you're edible."

My mind flashes back to all the times he ate me out during our night together, and an unwelcome flush creeps up my neck. I huff to cover up my discomfort. "I'm sure that's how he looks at anything with breasts."

Janie snorts. "He didn't look like that at me, and I have breasts."

That she does—and they're still natural, as far as I can tell, though she'll probably get a boob job soon.

Back in the day, I called Janie "Miss Natural" because she studiously avoided chemicals, fragrances, and dyes. Now, due to Mr. Suck-Up's influence, she looks like she's stepped out of one of Tierre's shoots. The only nod to her former self is the lack of perfume, but that is merely to appease Marcus, the person Mr. Suck-Up is dying to please.

"Did you know that tonight's dinner—and tomorrow's reception—will be prepared by a Michelin-starred chef?" she asks.

"No." And the Janie I knew never cared about things like Michelin stars; her main concern would've been whether the ingredients were non-GMO.

"I wonder which one," she muses. "Landon thinks it's one of Gordon Ramsay's students, or maybe even the man himself."

Right. Landon is her boyfriend's actual name. "Listen, Janie, I'm pretty beat after the flight. Can we catch up later?"

"Of course," she chirps. "See you at dinner."

Maybe. If Emma and Marcus aren't there, I won't be either.

I claim my room, which turns out to have a glorious ocean view and is bigger than my Manhattan apartment.

Watching the waves break against the golden sand, I call Emma to find out about dinner. Turns out, she and Marcus are visiting her grandparents and won't make it to the mansion until late.

That settles it. I'm going to order in some food. But first, I need to plan a proper vacation activity for after the wedding—because I told Mr. Boss the festivities would last four days, since I haven't had an actual holiday in ages.

The question is, what do I do with my free time?

It's February, so the ocean is going to be too cold for my liking despite the heatwave forecasted for the next couple of days. Nor am I into theme parks, especially if it's going to be in the upper 80s, as predicted. Though something nature-y might be nice, something unique to Florida.

I end up settling on Swamp Sparkle Safari, which is an overnight airboat tour that sounds amazing. According to their spiel, the owner takes you to a remote swamp location that only he knows about, and you get to experience bioluminescence and encounter gators cavorting with turtles, along with a firefly light show that accompanies a frog serenade.

"I'm sold," I tell the owner, Bubba, who picks up the phone when I call. "Book me for the day after tomorrow."

"You're not going to regret this," he says in a charming Southern accent. "The cabin where you'll be staying at just got renovated."

"Thanks. I'll see you soon."

I'm glad I planned for this. Even if I weren't desperate for a vacation, I'll need the relaxation after the hard work of being civil to Ashton.

Vacation plans arranged, I order Mexican takeout and deal with the numerous emails and texts from Tierre that piled up while I was offline.

Once my inbox is blissfully empty, I open Adobe Illustrator and stare at the screen, hoping for a visit from the design inspiration fairy—whom I picture looking like a hybrid between Tinkerbell and Tierre.

I feel like I might be on the verge of an idea, but then the chiming of the doorbell interrupts my musings and the inspiration vanishes. Annoyed, I get up and go to the front door to get my food.

"Here are your orders," the delivery guy says and gives me two bags, one heavier than the other.

"Orders, as in plural?"

"One of those is mine," Ashton says from behind me. "The one with shrimp tacos."

"Good choice." The guy points at the heavier of the two bags. "That would be that one."

Damn it. Now I want shrimp tacos. Mine are grilled steak and pork.

"Why are you ordering takeout?" I demand as soon as the delivery guy leaves.

"Because I figured you'd want to dine with your friend Janie."

I know this might be hypocritical given that I'm avoiding him, but the idea that he's avoiding *me* pisses me off.

"Fine. I guess I *will* join Janie and the rest of them."

"Go ahead," he says with infuriating magnanimousness. "I only know two people at that table, Geoffrey and Jarrod, and I'm not that close to either."

The names sound familiar.

Ah, right, one of them is Marcus's CIO and the other is his butler—not sure which is which.

"Have fun," he says, then turns around and leaves.

I locate the dining room and add my tacos to the pile of food already on the table.

Unlike Tierre, I don't believe in juju or the evil eye, but if I did, I'd be positive Ashton's "have fun" cursed this dinner because it turns out to be boring, awkward, and tedious, with Mr. Suck-Up telling us endless stories about Goldman Sachs, the investment bank where he works.

On the bright side, the stories manage to make me so drowsy I fall asleep as soon as I get to my room.

Unfortunately, the curse continues.

I'm bombarded by a variety of wet dreams, all of which feature Ashton.

CHAPTER 17

Kendall

A KNOCK on the door wakes me just as I'm sucking on Ashton's neck like a horny Nosferatu.

Turns out, Marcus hired a makeup artist for the bridal party. The woman is good too, as skilled as the pros we have at our shoots in New York. And she's thoughtful. She brings me breakfast and has me eat it as she works on my nails.

Freshly primped and preened, I exit my room and head outside, where I'm relieved to see that Marcus ordered two limos for us even though we could easily squeeze into one.

"Morning," says Janie.

"Morning," I say, giving her a quick onceover. She makes the bridesmaid dress look good, and I tell her so, eliciting a bright smile from her.

"Do you know which car Ashton's riding in?" I ask.

"He just got into that one," she says and points at the farthest limo. "Go ahead. There's still room."

"What about you?" I ask. "Which one will you take?"

She points to the nearer limo. "Landon wants to talk to Jarrod some more."

"Ah. I see." My choices seem to be Ashton or Mr. Suck-Up. "I'm going with you guys, so you and I can catch up."

She nods at that, but like during the dinner last night, we don't really get the chance to catch up because her boyfriend word-vomits business ideas to Jarrod the entire ride.

Exiting the limo, I take in our surroundings: a golden-sand beach in front of a rough, gray-blue ocean, with a few surfers bravely catching the tall-ish waves. A boardwalk stretches as far as the eye can see in either direction, and happy beachgoers frolic about, clearly enjoying the warm weather.

"That's where it will happen." Janie gestures at the pier in the middle of it all.

I figured as much, given the red carpet leading to our destination, and the fact that the pier has been heavily decorated with flowers and balloons.

"I thought everything was going to be super simple," I muse.

"And it is, simple… for a billionaire," she says.

She has a point. The red and white roses covering every empty inch of the pier likely cost more than I make in a year, but the flowers are not gold-plated, which shows definite restraint on Marcus's part.

"What's with the cat food jars?" Janie asks.

Huh. She's right. Right below each balloon is a can of cat food, all different brands.

I grin. "It's a nod to the first gift Marcus sent Emma —flowers and cat food."

What I don't add is that Janie would know this if she hadn't disappeared on us, resurfacing only because of her boyfriend's machinations.

No. I will not be negative today. Not on Ems's wedding day.

I will be so saintly I might even be nice to Ashton... Or if not nice, very good at avoiding conflict.

And... speak of the devil. I spot him, wearing a bespoke tux.

Holy fuck. The effect of Ashton's signature V-shape is multiplied a thousand-fold, and an air of old-money, commanding arrogance pours out of his every cufflink and lapel. And did I mention the confidence the suit makes him exude? It's radiating from him like a fucking halo.

Wait. What am I doing? I'm supposed to ignore the manwhore, not ogle him like a tasty morsel.

Yet, when he spots me, his eyes darken temptingly, and I can't help but lick my lips—a gesture that makes the asshole smirk, like he knows the effect he's having on me.

"Nice dress," he murmurs, approaching us.

Janie audibly gulps. "Are you talking to me?"

"Of course," he says, turning his potent charm on her. "Who else?"

Janie blushes.

Poor girl. Ashton in that tux has clearly jumbled her brain enough to forget that we're wearing the exact same dress.

And hey, I feel her pain… and wish I were wearing more substantial underwear.

Fuck.

The wedding.

Must focus on it.

Except Marcus and Emma aren't here. Nor is the priest—assuming that Marcus wants to use one to officiate, and not, say, an Ayn Rand impersonator or the Secretary of the Treasury.

Oh, I know. Maybe I should think about my design project. Would that make me stop darting glances at Ashton?

It's worth a shot, except I'm still a bit blank when it comes to the details of my project.

Maybe I should design a tuxedo? For women?

No. Too close to the thing that I'm trying to avoid.

A wedding dress?

Hmm. That's actually not a bad idea. Tierre has done this for a few celebs and—

"Hello, everyone," says a beautiful and much-too-cheerful woman holding a giant camera. "My name is Gala, and I'm the MC and photographer for this nuptial jubilee."

"Hi, Gala," Ashton says in that deep, melty voice of his.

"Hi," Gala answers breathlessly. Based on her

expression, something has clearly just short-circuited in her brain. Or her ovaries.

"Where do you want us?" Ashton asks.

Snapping out of her daze, Gala has all the groomsmen pose together, then the bridesmaids, and then it's time for what I've been dreading since she showed up: a group photo.

"I want you there." Gala points me right at Ashton's crotch.

I swallow hard and shake my head.

Ashton's eyes grow flinty, but he doesn't comment.

"Why not?" Gala asks. "Aren't you a couple?"

I gape at her. "What? No! What gave you that idea?"

She shrugs. "When you shoot weddings for as long as I have, you develop a knack for these things."

"Well, we're not," I snap.

"Can you stand together anyway?" She bats her eyelashes pleadingly at Ashton. "It would make the picture look more balanced."

Muttering something under his breath, Ashton walks over and stands by me, which makes me feel like a space object caught in the devastating gravitational pull of Jupiter. My palms sweat, and my heart pitter-patters in my chest as if I'm having a heart attack.

"No. There." Gala takes me by the shoulders and thrusts me right into Ashton.

Holy shit. There's an erection poking my ass.

What. The. Fuck? Does Ashton just walk around with a hard-on? Or did he sprout it just to bring forth that heart attack for real?

"Say 'conjugal,'" Gala squeaks.

Everyone does, but thanks to his proximity, Ashton's voice is like a purr in my ear... and it reverberates in my nipples.

"Thank you," Gala says. "I think I got it."

Thank God. I leap out of range of Ashton's cock and take a few steps down the pier, just in case it chases me.

I really don't want a heart attack right now. Or an orgasm.

"Hi, everyone," says a newcomer who's dressed like a priest. "The bride and groom are going to be here any minute, so please take your positions."

After some confusion, we're told where to stand, and it's pretty obvious in hindsight: bridesmaids on one side, groomsmen on the other.

A live band shows up, seemingly out of nowhere, and starts playing classical music, a melody I soon recognize as "Billionaire" by Travie McCoy.

I choke back a laugh. This is clearly Emma's idea of a joke. Then I see Ashton grinning, which ruins my mood.

Predictably, considering the song, Marcus walks down the aisle and stands in front of the priest—with Emma's grandmother at his side, which is so adorable my eyes get misty.

Smoothly, the band transitions into the traditional "Here Comes the Bride."

Everyone looks to the base of the pier as Emma appears in a magnificent Vera Wang ivory lace concoction that flatters her curves and makes her pale skin glow. Her hair, styled in a gorgeous updo, looks especially radiant with the sunlight shining on it. Her grandfather is escorting her down the aisle, a proud smile on his weathered face.

Damn it. I should've brought some water with me. Between my eyes leaking and the dampness in my panties from being next to Ashton earlier, I'm at risk of dehydration.

"Dearly beloved," the priest says and proceeds with the charming ceremony, the highlight of which is when one of Emma's cats walks down the aisle on a leash held by Marcus's butler. At first, I'm unclear as to why, but then I spot the little pillow attached to the cat's back.

The fuzzy furball is the ring bearer.

Actually, no. The highlight of the ceremony is when Emma and Marcus read their vows—because they are heartfelt and touching, and contribute further to my dehydration.

"—and now, I pronounce you man and wife," the priest concludes. Smiling at Marcus, he adds, "You may kiss the bride."

Oh, wow. The kiss Marcus gives my friend is of the type where, under any other circumstances, everyone would say "get a room." It's so passionate and possessive it makes me feel like a voyeur.

Flushing, I look away, only to have my gaze fall on Ashton's lips.

Shit.

Catching me looking at him, Ashton arches a questioning eyebrow.

I pretend to wipe a bead of sweat off my forehead… with my middle finger.

He slowly shakes his head and mouths, "Very mature."

Before I can pantomime a response, the newlyweds finally disconnect from their scorching kiss, and everyone claps.

"Time for more pictures!" Gala shouts and proceeds to usher us to the beach, where I manage to somehow steer clear of Ashton's cock.

"The cocktail hour and reception will be at the mansion," Gala tells us when she's done with the million pictures.

On the way there, I take the limo that Ashton isn't in, and I avoid drinking too much at cocktail hour because if I get drunk, I'm not sure I'll be able to stay civil… or keep my legs shut.

At the reception, I'm happy to learn that we're allowed to pick our seats, so I sit far, far away from Ashton, which helps me enjoy the scrumptious first course.

"Can I have your attention please," Gala says into the mic. "First, say hello to your band: The Wedding Smashers."

Said band begins playing their rendition of "I Gotta Feeling" by The Black-Eyed Peas, but instead of anyone singing, mid-way through, Gala announces, "And now, for the first time as husband and wife: Mr. and Mrs. Carelli."

The music grows louder, and Emma and Marcus make their grand entrance. Between her hair seeming a touch frizzy and Marcus's tie being askew, they look suspiciously like they've already consummated their marriage.

Their first dance starts, and if I thought their kiss was scorching, the way they sway together is the closest thing to sex in public that I've ever seen.

In fact, I'm shocked that they go to sit at their table afterward instead of sneaking out for a quickie.

Soon after the next course arrives, Emma's grandfather and grandmother each give a beautifully touching speech to celebrate the blissful newlyweds, and I thank the makeup gods above that I'm wearing waterproof mascara. After that, Gala demands that everyone head over to the dance floor.

Nope. Not doing it.

Everyone else goes to dance—that is, except Ashton, who's also stayed in his seat.

"That won't do," Gala says. "The two of you have to get out there."

I shake my head as a slow song starts playing.

"Please, Kendall." Emma's grandmother appears at my elbow to bat her eyelashes at me. "Just this one dance? Emma wants everyone to have a good time."

"Grandma, it's fine!" Emma calls from the dance floor.

Shit. Everyone is looking at me and Ashton instead

of at the bride and groom. This is precisely what I didn't want to happen. Ashton must be on the same wavelength because he stoically gets up and makes his way over to my table.

"Care to dance?" he drawls, extending his hand to me.

I don't exactly have a choice now, do I?

Clenching my teeth, I place my hand in his and do my best to ignore the sparks racing up my arm as he leads me to the dance floor.

Once we reach our destination, he pulls me to him, and air whooshes out of my lungs as we end up in the classic slow-dance position: his left hand holding my right, his other hand on the bare skin just below my shoulder blades, and last but not least, his erection against my belly.

"What do you think you're doing?" I whisper so that only he can hear.

He leans down, and his lips brush my ear as he whispers back, "This is a slow dance. I'm holding you in a traditional style. What else did you expect me to do?"

"I expected you to have the decency to get rid of *that*," I whisper-hiss, keeping my voice even quieter as I direct my glare to the offending appendage.

"My apologies, fashionista. Whenever you're around, I have very little control over *that*."

That's a compliment, right? Same as if I told him that his proximity is making my nipples pebble, and my—

No. Must think unsexy thoughts, like a wedding cake stuffed with sardines, pickles, and spicy mayo. Or a bowl of worms with spaghetti sauce. Or a room full of zombies that have spinach in their teeth.

Nope. Doesn't work. The more we sway to the music, the more I want to strip that tux from Ashton's shoulders and—

The slow song stops. Ashton gently releases me and steps back, his expression unreadable.

Damn him and damn this stupid dance. Now I miss his touch, and that's insane.

"Thank you, I'm going to my seat now," I say loudly enough for Ashton—and more importantly, Emma and her grandmother—to hear. "I'm starving."

Ashton nods mockingly. "I understand. I'm ravenous myself."

Nostrils flaring, I turn on my heel and stride back to my seat, feeling very proud not to have yelled or otherwise created a scene.

The problem is, I'm still too turned on to enjoy the rest of the evening. I can't even properly taste the wedding cake that the chef made to look like the chandelier hanging above us. All I can do is sneak glances at Ashton and curse myself for being so susceptible to a good-looking—okay, make that gorgeous—asshole.

"Okay, ladies and gentlemen," Gala says after the cake is distributed. "The newlyweds can't seem to wait to start their married life, so they're headed for their bedroom."

Emma blushes crimson, Marcus grins, and everyone makes inappropriate jokes, even Emma's grandparents.

As the happy couple head down the corridor toward the master suite, the band starts playing one of Tierre's favorite songs by AC/DC: "You Shook Me All Night Long."

CHAPTER 18

Ashton

AFTER THE NEWLYWEDS LEAVE, the reception winds down. Emma's grandparents leave next, followed by a few of the younger guests. Since I'm staying here at the mansion, I don't rush to my room. Instead, I chew the lamp from the chandelier cake and ponder an important question: Why do boner pill commercials tell you to visit the ER if an erection lasts longer than four hours? I hope that directive only applies *after* you've taken a boner pill. Because when I'm around Kendall—which I have been for more than four hours today—I'm hard almost all the time, so if I'm doing some permanent damage to my dick, it would be nice to know that.

Speaking of Kendall, she gets up from her seat, says farewell to a bunch of people, pointedly ignores me, and heads out, hips swaying from side to side, sending even more blood to my dick.

Fuck. Me. Why do I have this reaction toward the

one woman who's gotten it into her head to hate me? Is this some sort of fetish?

Just as I'm about to throw caution to the wind and follow her out, I hear a soft feminine voice say, "Hi," yanking my brain back to reality.

I turn and see that it's the photographer/MC, except she's not holding the camera or the mic.

"Hey." I scooch my chair deeper under the table to hide my Kendall-induced erection. "What's up?"

Damn. Bad choice of words, all things considered.

The woman smiles. "You're Ashton, right?"

I nod. "And you're Gala?"

"Yes." Her eyes gleam with delight. "That's me…" She looks at me expectantly.

"You did a great job hosting the event," I say. "And I can't wait for those pictures." Especially the one where Kendall's butt was on my crotch.

Gala blinks rapidly, like a pretty owl. "I came over to tell you that I'm going to be off the clock in just a few minutes…"

"Oh. That's great." Is she propositioning me? Didn't she tell me a few hours ago that Kendall and I had a vibe? Or is that what got her interested?

"Yeah. So…" She moistens her glossy lips. "I was wondering if you wanted to talk… afterward?"

Damn. She *is* looking for a fuck. I'm certain of it now. And she's a great-looking woman, so considering that I'm a warm-blooded male with a hard-on problem, I should be jumping for joy.

I surprise all three of us—Gala, myself, and my cock

—when I say, "I actually have to call my girlfriend in a few minutes."

Given Gala's grimace, I wasn't exactly subtle. But she doesn't question why I didn't bring my imaginary girlfriend as a plus one, and in general, she recovers quickly.

Thrusting a business card into my hand, she says, "Take this. If you and your girlfriend decide to tie the knot, I'd love to host your wedding."

"I'll keep that in mind. Thank you."

She takes a step back. "I'm going to network some more. That's what I was doing, by the way."

"Of course. Good luck."

She heads toward Jarrod, and my cock demands to know why the fuck I just turned down such an opportunity. I mean, we both know it was either Gala or my hand tonight—or else I won't be able to sleep. And my cock is very tired of my hand because that's all he's known for the past three years.

And no. The lack of female company had nothing to do with Kendall and our way-too-memorable night together. I've just been busy with my business and haven't met the right woman.

The music stops. Gala announces that she and the band are finished for the evening, and so is the open bar—but that all are welcome to hang out as long as we want.

After saying my goodbyes to the people still in the ballroom, I head to my room. The thought that is front and center on my mind for the second night in a row is that Kendall is sleeping under the same roof. She's naked (in my fantasy at least) only a few steps away, her long legs—

Groaning in frustration, I enter my bathroom and angrily fist my dick.

There. Maybe now I can get some sleep.

I WAKE UP JUST AS THE SUN IS BEGINNING TO RISE. Despite the early hour, I feel wide awake.

Fucking great. There goes my chance to sleep in on a rare day free of business meetings and client sessions.

Oh, well. I put on a pair of boxers and go to my balcony to watch the sunrise and do a bodyweight workout, followed by some yoga and a hot shower.

Okay, so maybe waking up early wasn't so bad. Once the sun is up all the way, I dress and head to the kitchen to rummage through the fridge for some breakfast. Then I return to my room and stalk Kendall's social media—purely because, as Sun Tzu famously said, "Know your enemy."

Eventually, I realize how crazy what I'm doing is, so I try to think of something else to do, something where I'm unlikely to bump into her.

The beach is out because that's where most people are probably going to be.

Maybe a jet ski tour?

No. If I do bump into her there, she'll be wearing a bikini, and that way lies madness.

But I like the idea of a water activity. Maybe

something on a boat? And maybe where I can see some wildlife?

I do some searching until I find a winner: Swamp Sparkle Safari.

That's it. A swamp is the last place a fashionista would want to be, but to me, this seems like a perfect way to spend the day.

In another life, I might've enjoyed being a survivalist, making fire by focusing the sun's rays through a water bottle and living off roasted squirrels.

I book the tour, and the owner, Bubba, tells me I got the last of the two "coveted" spots.

Bubba, who greets me when I show up for the tour, reminds me of a swamp-dwelling version of Captain Jack Sparrow from *Pirates of the Caribbean*, with alligator teeth weaved into his orange dreadlocks, camo clothes, and a bull's skull belt buckle that's large enough to impale a cow.

"How's your momma and em?" Bubba asks after he gives me a very thorough handshake.

"Good?" I glance at the two boats nearby. "How are things with you?"

"It's fixin' to be a good day," Bubba says. "Today's I'm gonna ask my darlin' to be my wife." He gestures at the hut that serves as the office of Swamp Sparkle Safari. "Just don't tell her when she gives you your paperwork."

At that moment, a woman comes out of the hut, holding a piece of paper. She's wearing a dress made out of the same camo material as Bubba's outfit, and her face is hidden by a beekeeper mask. To deter mosquitos, maybe?

"G'day, mate," she says with an Australian accent. "Alligator Dottie is my name. Giving tours that blow your mind is my game." She thrusts the paper into my hands. "But first, sign the waiver."

According to the paper, Swamp Sparkle Safari LLC is not responsible for gators eating any parts of the signee, or the signee having an allergic reaction to ticks or mosquito bites, or the signee getting rat lungworm after eating a raw apple snail.

Hmm. "Was that last one based on something that happened?" I ask Dottie as I sign.

She nods. "And I told her, deep fry the critter, but she didn't listen, and then later died of eosinophilic meningitis."

"Right. Okay. Raw apple snails are off the menu."

"It seems like you're ready," Dottie says. "Now go ahead, jump into my boat."

"Hold up a minute," Bubba drawls. "I've had a change of heart." He looks at me, then at Dottie, and then at me again. "I'll take him, and you take the other client."

"Why?" Dottie asks. "You don't trust me with this spunk?"

Is that an Australian compliment?

"I trust ya but…" I can see him thinking, hard. "It's just that the other client sounded fancy pants. She might feel more comfortable getting a ride from a lady."

"All right." Dottie takes the paper from me. "Have a ripper of a time."

CHAPTER 19

Kendall

"HEY, MATE, CHECK THAT OUT." Dottie gestures in the direction of a nearby cypress tree.

Whoa. A horny deer—in multiple senses of that word—is mounting a doe, and they are going at it. Hard. There are sound effects and everything, particularly from the male, with the noise resembling some horrid combination of belching, groaning, snoring, growling, and snorting.

Is that how the seven dwarves got their names? Snow White saw some deer making a beast with two backs and horns?

"It's rare to see the rut here in the swamp," Dottie says. "You're lucky."

Yeah, for some unknown reason, I don't actually feel all that lucky. In fact, I could've gone my whole life without ever witnessing how Bambis are made—or hearing the word "rut" used in a sentence.

"I hope a gator doesn't eat them," I say.

We saw some disturbingly large members of that species earlier, including one that was at least ten feet long.

"No worries, mate. Gators only chow down on fawns or the ones that are a bit crook."

"Ah." I figure someone who goes by "Alligator Dottie" would know such things. I swat at my millionth mosquito in the last hour. "How far are we from the secret island?"

"Oh, no worries, mate. You've got many more hours of the tour to enjoy."

Great. I'm going to arrive at our destination as an exsanguinated husk.

"THOUGHTS?" DOTTIE ASKS AS WE FINALLY PULL UP TO A small pier on the secret island.

"If I don't see another gator for the rest of my life, I think I'll be perfectly happy," I say, heroically fighting the urge to scratch at my mosquito bites.

Dottie chuckles and tells me the real treat starts when it gets dark because there will be frogs singing, fireflies lighting up the place, and—the highlight of it all —the swamp around us glowing with bioluminescence.

"Yeah. That sounds really cool," I say.

I'm hoping this experience will somehow inspire my designs.

"She'll be right," she says, which at this point, I recognize as Australian for, "It will be."

"Sugah Roo!" a weird-looking dude yells as he comes out of the cabin farthest from us.

"Bubba!" Dottie shouts giddily.

She flies into his arms, and he lifts her beekeeper-net-like veil and gives her a kiss that reminds me of the deer in rut.

When they eventually stop the PDA, Dottie introduces Bubba as her boyfriend—as though I couldn't have guessed that part.

"Your cabin's waitin' for ya." Bubba gestures at the cabin that's nearer the water. "Why don't you go check it out while Dottie and I go on a pleasure ride?"

"Sure." Pleasure ride? Please, for the love of my libido, spare me the details.

Dottie thrusts a walkie-talkie into my hands, instructs me to call if I need anything, and then they sprint toward the pier like two horny teens. And I'm not talking the deer variety.

Hopping into the boat I just rode in, they torpedo away.

"What the fuck?" says a familiar voice from the doorway of the more inland cabin.

No.

Can't be.

This has to be a swamp-induced hallucination, like when people see fairies in this kind of environment, or —given that we're in Florida—the Skunk Ape.

"What the fuck right back at you," I say to Ashton—because that's whom I see, wearing a pair of shorts and a sleeveless T-shirt that exposes way too many of his perfectly defined muscles.

Unlike me, he doesn't seem to be covered with mosquito bites. Which tracks. They probably avoid evil.

"Seriously, what are you doing here?" Ashton demands. "And where did they just take that boat?"

"I'm on a tour, which I assume is what *you're* doing. And Bubba said they're going on a pleasure ride." I surreptitiously rub my eyes, but Ashton is still there afterward.

"Pleasure ride? What a load of bullshit. He told me he was going to propose to his girlfriend today—but I didn't realize he'd need to strand me here to do so."

"Strand us." I take the walkie-talkie and press the push-to-talk button. "Hey, Dottie, I need you to come back. There's been a misunderstanding."

No one replies.

I press the button again. "Dottie, this is not a joke. Come back immediately."

"I think that thing is dead," Ashton says.

Fuck. I'm afraid he's right. There's no sign of a charge left in the stupid device.

I pull out my phone.

Double fuck. Zero bars.

"Can you fix this?" I thrust the walkie-talkie into Ashton's hands.

He turns it around and opens the battery compartment. "Do you have two AA batteries?"

"Only back in New York." It's what powers my

vibrator—a device I've missed dearly on this trip, and it's all his fault.

Ashton hands the walkie-talkie back. "Sounds like we have to wait for the lovebirds to get back."

"No. Fuck that." I run toward the boat they left behind.

"What's the idea?" he asks from behind me. "You're going to steal their boat?"

"Borrow," I throw over my shoulder.

"And then what? Do you actually remember the way back?"

"Yes." Not really, but I don't remember much zigzagging, so I bet if I go straight in roughly the right direction, I'll get back to some kind of land.

Reaching the boat, I jump inside and look for a way to start it.

"It needs a key," Ashton says, joining me inside. "But even if you magically produced it, I'd still say this is a bad idea."

"Get off my boat," I snap.

"How is this suddenly *your* boat?"

"You're happy to stay back and wait. That means I'm the one sailing away."

"Except you're not."

Ignoring him, I scour the boat for a key, but to no avail.

"Maybe it can be jump-started with wires?" I examine the panel skeptically.

"Sure. Why don't you pull up a YouTube tutorial?"

I pull my phone out and then realize why he

sounded so smug: no reception means no YouTube. Fucking technology.

"Do *you* have service?" I demand.

He takes out his phone and shows me that he has no bars either.

My heart sinks. "Is there Wi-Fi in the cabins?"

He snorts. "A better question is: is there electricity?"

I gape at him. "You're kidding, right?"

He shakes his head. "I didn't see any light switches or bulbs, and I doubt they provided those matches and candles for ambience's sake."

"Fuck."

"Relax, fashionista." He sounds annoyingly calm. "He'll propose, and they'll come back. Meanwhile, you can stay in your cabin, and I in mine."

"Great idea." I kick the side of the cockpit. "I'll do just that."

Hopping out of the boat, I stomp toward my cabin, and as if to match my mood, dark clouds begin to gather overhead.

CHAPTER 20
Ashton

I'M SO angry the room around me darkens.

As usual, Kendall is un-fucking believable. Of all the things she could've done, she had to crash my swamp getaway and then give me that attitude. Like this clusterfuck is my fault.

If anything, *she* was the one who let the lovebirds get away. If I thought even for a second that Bubba had planned to leave for his proposal, I would've stopped him, with fists if necessary.

A booming clap of thunder rattles the cabin.

Shit. I guess the room didn't darken because of my anger.

Heavy raindrops start drumming on the wooden roof.

Just perfect. Now I can't even take a stroll around this stupid island.

As I fume, the rain intensifies, and the visibility

worsens so much I have to light the candles that are sitting in the candelabra on the table.

Shit. Kendall must be freaking out.

The urge to go check on her is strong, but I resist because if she wanted my company, she would be here. At least that's what I tell myself for the next hour or so, but then a bolt of lightning illuminates my room, followed by an immediate thunderclap.

Fuck. I'm not an expert, but I seem to recall that if you see lightning and hear thunder soon after, the hit was nearby.

What if it hit Kendall's cabin?

Leaping to my feet, I open the door.

Wow. I thought we were in the middle of a swamp, not the depths of Mordor.

I strain to make out if there's smoke coming from Kendall's cabin as wind and rain pelt my face, but I can't see shit.

I need to get closer.

Abandoning the dry safety of the cabin, I propel myself into the storm, my sneakers squelching and my instantly soaked clothes clinging to my body like leeches.

As I get closer to Kendall's cabin, I see that the lightning didn't strike it, but she needs a rescue anyway.

Crossing the distance, I knock on the door.

Kendall opens it, looking pale. "What do you want?"

"Come. Quick."

"Where?" she demands. "And why?"

"My cabin," I tell her. "Because flash flood."

Her eyes widen. "Where?"

I point at the rising water near the shore.

Assessing the situation, she turns even paler. "Let me get my stuff."

"I'm not sure how much time you have." The muddy muck is just a few feet away from us and approaching fast.

Without reply, she disappears into her cabin.

Fuck.

I go after her, just in time to see her put a plastic bag with socks into her backpack.

"Take only the necessities," I snap, then grab a heap of nearby clothing and shove it into her bag.

"Fine." She shoulders the backpack. "Let's go."

Working on pure instinct, I grab the blanket on the bed and cover her with it as best as I can, then grip her hand. "Let's run."

To punctuate my words, water seeps from under the door to the cabin.

Kendall must comprehend the urgency of our situation because she doesn't jerk her hand away or say anything as we do our best to run.

The going is tough as we wade through water up to our ankles near her cabin, but it gets easier once we're more uphill.

"Do you think the water will reach here?" Kendall pants as we burst into my cabin.

"I doubt it." But just in case, I locate the stairwell to the attic. "If anything, we go up there," I tell her.

"And what if—"

"I'm a great swimmer," I say as reassuringly as I can. "I'll get us to that boat. Even without the keys, the thing floats, so we should be okay." Hopefully.

She looks me over. "You're dripping."

"So are you." I gesture at her backpack. "Do you have anything you can change into? Or do you want to borrow something of mine?" Even if that something are the only dry items I have left.

She takes her backpack off her shoulders. "I've got pajamas."

"Good. I'll turn around and go change in that corner while you change here." I grab my stuff and do just that, then loudly ask if she's decent.

"Yeah. You can turn back."

When I do, she's wearing a black silk slip that reveals enough of her milky flesh for me to get hard instantly despite the apocalypse raging outside.

Her feet are bare, with a neat taupe-colored nail polish that looks to have been painted two seconds ago, and she's wearing two silvery toe rings and a golden anklet. Said jewelry aside, hers are the prettiest feet I've ever seen, and I've never been into feet—until this moment, that is. I want to suck on her—

She shivers, making me feel like an insensitive asshole.

"Are you cold?" I ask gently, coming toward her. This being Florida, the inside of the non-air-conditioned cabin feels pretty balmy, but I have more of my skin covered—especially in the leg area.

"Yes. No. I don't know." She walks over to the wooden bed and sits on the edge. "Can you… hold me?"

"Of course." Even if that means my balls become bluer than a Smurf's.

Moving softly so I don't spook her further, I sit and gently wrap my arm around her trembling shoulders.

"We're going to be okay," I whisper.

A violent thunderclap chooses that very moment to crack angrily in the distance.

Kendall jerks in response. "How can you know that?"

I pull her closer. "Nothing is going to happen to you." I won't let it.

"I guess. But… just in case… can we take a break?"

I face her, forehead furrowing. "What do you mean?"

Her hazel eyes gleam in the candlelight. "Can we not hate each other? Just for a few minutes." She dampens her soft lips. "If we're going to die—"

"We're not."

"But if," she insists. "I don't want—"

"I don't hate you," I say truthfully. "I might've been disappointed when you ghosted me, but—"

She puts a finger to my lips. "That. Let's take a break from all that… in case…"

I feather-kiss that finger. "There's no 'in case,' fashionista. I promise you."

"Not arguing is part of the proposed break," she mutters. "Please."

"Okay."

She stares at me, her finger still hovering over my lips, and on impulse, I lean in and suck it in. She gasps, her eyes widening, but then her other hand lands on my thigh and moves just a fraction to brush against my aching cock.

I bite back a groan and gently release her finger.

"Kendall…"

She swallows, and her hand moves more decisively, rubbing over my erection.

I can't hold back the groan this time. "Fuck… are you sure you know what you're doing?" Because if this is just because she's scared, I don't want her to hate me even more for taking advantage. That is, I badly want to take advantage, but—

"I think so," she whispers, eyes darkening. "Do you have a condom?"

Fuuuck. "No. But… I'm clean." I dare not even hope she's on the pill and willing to—

"I'm clean too and have an IUD," she says breathlessly. "Not that it matters if—"

"If you say we're about to die, I will not fuck you," I say thickly, though it's a huge bluff.

I'd fuck her even if the swamp were currently engulfing us—and I'd drown a happy man.

"Okay." She bites her lip and flinches as another clap of thunder shakes the cabin. Her voice is husky. "Then do it as a distraction. Make me forget."

"That I can do." I pull her to me, growling into her ear, "In fact, I will fuck you so hard you'll think the sun is shining."

CHAPTER 21

Kendall

AS SOON AS Ashton's lips clash with mine, the outside world fades away, and my already-racing pulse goes into overdrive.

His tongue invades my mouth, a prelude for what I want his cock to do. My inner muscles clench, and to call what I am wet would not do my condition justice.

I'm soaking.

Needy.

Greedy for him.

Ripping desperately at his clothes, I free his magnificent erection while he peels my slip from me.

"Glorious," he rasps, cupping my left breast.

"Don't get distracted," I say breathlessly.

Nostrils flaring, he captures my nipples—the right one with his mouth, the left with his fingers.

Holy crap. Can you come from attention to the nipples? Because I feel on the verge of doing just that, but then his erection presses against my sex, and *that* makes me almost come as well.

"You're positive you want this?" The question seems to require Ashton to possess an impossible level of self-control.

In reply, I grip his cock and guide him to my entrance, where I'm desperate for it.

His blue-gray eyes are molten as they peer into mine. Slowly, he pushes into me, allowing my muscles to adjust to his girth.

No. That's not what I need. "Faster."

With an animalistic grunt, he thrusts all the way.

Yes.

Fuck, yes.

"Harder." My nails dig into his back, punctuating my demand.

He responds by pistoning into me savagely, the expression on his face that of a starving beast.

Holy fuck. "I'm coming…"

His thrusts intensify.

I dig my nails deeper into his skin as my toes curl and I come so hard white specks dance in my vision. It's as if lightning has struck my clit and electrified all of my nerve endings.

Without giving me a chance to catch my breath, he keeps going with a hard, steady rhythm that pushes his pelvis against mine at just the right angle, hitting my pulsing clit and making another orgasm coil in my core.

I moan as his pace picks up, and then he grunts

thickly and thrusts one final time, so deeply I gasp. I feel him spill inside me, and I go over the edge, crying out his name before we collapse into a tangled heap of naked limbs on the bed.

By the time my panting breaths slow, everything seems quiet.

Too quiet.

"Is the thunderstorm over?" I demand indignantly.

Ashton languidly rises from the bed and peeks out the window. "Yeah. It's just drizzling now."

Shit. It's really over? But that means we're going to live. I know it's crazy to be disappointed by that, but I almost am.

If we're going to survive, I might've just made the biggest mistake of my life.

At least if I don't count sleeping with Ashton three years ago as that.

Ignoring the soreness between my legs, I leap to my feet, pull on my pajamas, and look around. "Where's the bathroom?"

He gives me a pitying look. "There isn't one. Not in the way you mean. There's an outhouse nearby." He gestures at the door.

I gape at him. "What about water? I need to wash up."

"Ah." He walks over to his backpack, takes out a towel, and wets it from a giant water cooler bottle in one corner of the room. "I hope this will suffice."

"Hardly," I snap. "And it goes without saying: I'm leaving Swamp Sparkle Safari a one-star review."

He nods. "I might go a step further and show Bubba some martial arts moves that I know."

"Right, assuming Bubba or Dottie ever come back." And hey, if they don't, we still might die here—so there's that.

As I take the towel from Ashton, my treacherous body reacts to his very naked nearness, but in my body's defense, he's semi-hard, again. And exuding heat. And smelling like a sex god.

"Turn away," I say imperiously.

He smirks. "I've already seen all there is to see."

"Please. Don't make this worse."

"Fine." He shows me his back, and I quickly wash up, then inform him that I'm done.

"So…" he says. "What now?"

My stomach rumbles. "Is there any food?"

He walks over to the water cooler bottle and gestures at a big jar near it. "I hope you like trail mix."

"I haven't had it since I was twelve." I go over there, grab a handful, and eat the nuts and seeds first, followed by the dried fruit and M&Ms.

"I like to eat it all together," Ashton says and demonstrates with a handful.

Fuck. I just came twice, so why am I finding that so erotic?

"Can you put some clothes on?" I ask when he swallows.

"If you insist." He drags his sweatpants up his long legs and covers his muscled torso with the shirt he was wearing—and I kind of regret losing sight of it all.

To distract myself, I grab another handful of trail mix. "How long can we survive on this?"

He frowns. "We don't need to survive on this at all. Bubba and Dottie will come back soon, I'm sure."

"Just hypothetically. Suppose they were on their boat when the weather changed, and something happened to them."

"You sure like to keep things light and positive. But fine. That looks like a two-gallon jug, which means thirty-two cups of trail mix." Squinting, he examines the label on the back of the jug. "It would take between two and four cups of the mix to provide us with enough calories for a day, so in the worst case, we have four days' worth of food—or double that if there's a jar just like this one in your cabin." He then gestures at the water bottle. "This thing is five gallons. We need about one gallon per day per person. Again, if your cabin has the same thing—which is likely—then it's about five days. And that's if we're determined to be well hydrated and fed. If we ration it..." He shrugs.

Crap. "I guess we really won't die. I told Emma where I was going, so if she doesn't hear from me for that long, she'll call the cops."

"There you go," he says. "We will survive." He starts to hum the famous Gloria Gaynor song, and I don't feel like telling him that the lyrics say "*I* will survive," not "we."

"Want to go for a walk?" I ask on impulse.

If we stay here, I'm afraid we're going to end up in bed again, and that sounds like a horrible idea.

He glances at my bare feet. "Like that?"

"No. I'll wear my wet shoes." I match actions to words, and he does the same.

"Yuck," he says as he takes the first squelchy step.

"Yeah, it's not pleasant."

We walk out into the fresh air, and much to my surprise, the sky is clear, without even a drizzle of rain.

In fact, there are no clouds at all, revealing the stars in a way you'd never see in a city.

I hear a chorus of frogs in the distance.

And, as if they'd been saving their energy for this very moment, a swarm of fireflies emerges from the swampy woods, forming a majestic display of light as they fade and brighten like twinkling stars.

"Wow," Ashton says. "Look." He points at the swamp.

Wow, indeed. The highly advertised bioluminescence illuminates the water, forming a mirror image of the night sky above and creating a beautiful and romantic atmosphere, especially when combined with the frog song, the stars overhead, and the overzealous fireflies.

"Okay, make it two stars," I tell him. "Maybe three."

We walk toward my cabin in utter awe.

The only damper on the romantic atmosphere is the mud surrounding my cabin. Well, that and the fact that I don't want to be in a romantic atmosphere with Ashton.

"You think I can sleep in there?" I ask as we approach.

He grimaces. "It probably smells like a moldy armpit."

"Thanks for that pleasant imagery. I'd like to check anyway." Because the alternative is his cabin, which only has one bed.

"Fine." He rolls his sweatpants up. "If you insist."

We make our way in, and it doesn't take me long to decide that sleeping in the flooded cabin is a no-go. I don't know why the swamp smells like something rotten, but it's so bad that I'm bound to wake up in the company of vultures.

"It does have sustenance." I point at the giant bottle and the jar that's exactly like the ones in his cabin. Walking over, I grab a few pieces of the trail mix. "The food is dry."

"I told you, we have plenty already," he says. "Now can we leave before we suffocate from the stink?"

"Yeah." I let him lead me out, and we walk slowly, enjoying the fresh air and the atmosphere once again.

"See? The boat seems fine." He gestures toward the pier.

"Let's hope the one they left on is doing just as well," I say, not convinced.

He clasps my hand in his big palm, sending zings through my veins. "All will be well. I promise."

"You can't know a thing like that." I know I should pull my hand away, but I can't bring myself to do so. It just feels too nice.

"Can we talk about something else?" he says.

"Sure. Like what?"

He lets my hand go and faces me. "Like the big question..."

My heartbeat picks up. "What question?" But I think I know what it is.

His blue-gray eyes glint with steel as he confirms my hunch. "Why did you ghost me?"

CHAPTER 22

Ashton

SHE STEPS BACK. "Is now really a good time to talk about this?"

I gesture around us. "We're not going anywhere anytime soon. When would it be a better time?"

She sighs. "We might be stuck here for a while, and discussing this will only make us more at odds with each other."

"We're already at odds with each other," I say. "Especially you with me for some unfathomable reason."

"Fine." She bites her lower lip, making my cock twitch. "The morning after we first... met, I learned how much you cat around."

I furrow my eyebrows. "Cat around?"

She scowls. "I learned how much you fuck different women. Is that clearer?"

Shit. That *was* one of my leading theories. But... "How?"

She shrugs. "Spoke to one of your 'conquests.' Her reviews were glowing, by the way. Five stars all around."

Fuck. Must be someone from college. "I wish you'd talked to me instead of just disappearing."

"Oh?" She lifts her chin. "Why is that?"

"Because I would've told you that it's all long behind me."

She folds her arms across her chest. "Yeah, right."

I put my hand over my heart. "After that time with you, I haven't been with anyone else."

She gapes at me, then snorts. "Bullshit. There's no way."

I grit my teeth. "Why would I lie?"

She shrugs. "To make me feel safer about having slept with you?"

I blow out a breath. "You *should* feel perfectly safe. Hell, I'll show you my clean bill of sexual health as soon as there's internet."

She waves that away. "Just because you never caught an STD doesn't mean you didn't stick a condom-shielded cock into every hole in Manhattan."

I pinch the bridge of my nose. "If you had bothered to get to know me, you wouldn't be saying all this."

Is that a glimmer of doubt in her eyes?

"Listen," she says. "Who you sleep with—or not—isn't any of my business. It was just… I felt like there was something between us that day, and when that woman told me about your 'situation', I felt—"

"But again," I say insistently. "What she told you is something that's in the past."

She scoffs. "How would you have felt if our roles were reversed? If some guy had told you I—"

"Short of learning that you were a sex worker or something, I would've spoken to you."

Her expression reminds me of the recent storm. "So... sleeping with a training client, you don't consider that sex work? More importantly, if *I* were a sex worker, you would've ghosted me?"

Why do women like to trap men with such hypotheticals? This is just like when an ex-girlfriend asked if I would've slept with Marilyn Monroe—and then started a huge fight with me because I said yes.

"If some guy told me such a thing about you, I'd give you the benefit of the doubt," I say carefully.

More like I would've beaten the truth out of the fucker, but we don't need to get into that.

Her eyes turn into slits. "And if you knew that I was, without any doubt?"

Deeper into hypotheticals? What's next: If we got married and I suffocated as I was giving you the best blow job in history, would you remarry? "I guess in such a scenario, I would have a problem with your job," I tell her.

"Is that so?"

"If you were mine, I would not share you with anyone else," I say with finality.

She narrows her eyes. "What if I needed the money?"

Seriously? "There are other hypothetical ways to make money."

"You sound just like a pampered Vancroft," she says, words dripping with disdain. "You've clearly never had to work for anything in your life. Everything's been handed to you on a silver platter."

I glare at her. "I've worked my ass off for what I have."

"Ass? Are you sure it wasn't your dick?"

My jaw ticks. "I think you've gotten so used to hating me that you're just looking for any excuse to do so."

"More like someone doesn't like the truth."

I blow out a frustrated breath. "What truth?"

"That your family is old money," she states. "And didn't you complain about the 'revenue growth' of your business—like it's a bad thing?"

"You don't know what the fuck you're talking about," I say.

My family cut me off when I dropped out of business school and chose my own path in life. What I've made of my business I've done on my own. If it were up to my parents, I'd be married to Gwyneth and working for my father. Do I hate it that my choice inadvertently led to riches? Yes, I do—because it's made my parents far too happy and proud of me.

Money is how they measure a person's worth in life, and I've finally become worthy in their eyes. But that's neither here nor there.

"I looked up the Bryces, you know," I tell Kendall.

"Your family is doing far too well for you to have a chip on your shoulder."

Kendall's father is a doctor, and her mother stays at home and volunteers at charities—which is the exact setup of Gwyneth's parents, I suddenly realize.

Such a little hypocrite, condemning *me* for having come from money.

As she glares at me, I ask tauntingly, "Are you telling me your father doesn't help you financially?"

She draws back, stiffening. "How do you know? You stalked me or something?"

"Emma mentioned something to Marcus about the financial help. The rest was on your social media."

Which I do not scroll through several times a day. Not at all.

Her lip curls. "Well, aren't you just the PI."

Uh-huh. "And how did you learn about *my* family?"

"Talking to you is too tiring. I'm going to bed."

She turns on her heel and strides away.

"Where the hell are you going?" I demand.

"I'll take my chances sleeping in the stinky cabin." She tries to slam the door, but the water damage makes that impossible.

Folding my arms across my chest, I stand there and wait.

If my recollection of the stench serves me right, she'll come out in twenty seconds—tops.

Nope.

With a banshee scream, Kendall flies out of her

cabin in *two* seconds—and to my shock, she runs over and hides behind me.

"What the hell?" I face her.

"A toad," she breathes. "Fat, warty, and with razor-sharp fangs."

I grin, unable to hide my amusement. "Toads don't have teeth, let alone fangs. They swallow their food alive, without chewing."

She shudders. "Was that supposed to sound reassuring?"

My grin widens. "You're too big for a toad to swallow."

She shakes her head vehemently. "That was a humongous toad. He probably grew up near a nuclear power plant."

"So… does this mean we're sharing my cabin?"

She looks at the evil toad's cabin and then at me. "I'll stay with you," she says reluctantly. "But no more sex."

"Sure. No sex… unless you ask for it."

I don't add "again," but the way her eyes shoot daggers at me means she remembers how things went down the last time.

"And clothes stay on," she says stubbornly.

"You can do what you want," I tell her. "I sleep naked, and that's when air conditioning *is* available."

"Fine. Just stay on your side of the bed."

With that, she turns toward my cabin and sashays away—which, given the thin slip that she's wearing, gives me a view so erotic I instantly regret agreeing to the "no sex" bit.

By the time I catch up with her, she's in bed, covered by a thin blanket.

I surreptitiously check the time on my phone.

Nine p.m. There's no way I'm going to fall asleep so early. Then again, besides that which she said is off the table, there's nothing else to do.

I take my clothes off, and I can feel her watching me as I do.

Getting under the blanket, I stay firmly on my side of the bed. I can smell apple and hibiscus, and just knowing she's near is making me painfully hard.

"Sweet dreams," I say, and my voice is more than a little raspy.

She doesn't reply, but I know she's awake.

Oh, well. She needs to process everything she's learned today.

Hell, I should do that also. First of all, should I forgive her for ghosting me, given what she said?

It's tempting. When she's not picking a fight with me, I like her very much—and the sexual chemistry between us is out of control. But... what if she didn't tell me the complete truth?

What if she didn't *just* ghost me because of what she learned, but also because I was a lowly personal trainer?

Her breathing evens out.

Damn. That's impressive. She fell asleep this early? She must have been tired.

My cock twitches, as if to remind me of what could've tired Kendall out.

Fuck. I doubt I'll fall asleep anytime soon, especially not with such a hard-on.

Maybe I can do something about it? Not here in bed —that would be creepy. Maybe outside? No. The last thing I want is a mosquito bite on my privates.

Suddenly, Kendall rolls over and drapes her arm over my chest.

Well, then. Unless I'm willing to wake her, it doesn't seem like I'm going anywhere. Especially not when she wraps more of herself over me, her breasts brushing my arm through her slip, and her right hand falling an inch away from my throbbing erection.

Is she actually asleep? Because if she wanted to torture me in some sort of revenge, she couldn't have come up with a better methodology.

"Ashton," she softly moans.

"Seriously?" I say out loud.

Her eyelashes flutter open, and her eyes widen. "Am I still dreaming?"

Fuck… "You dreamed about me?"

She looks at the tent that my erection is creating in the blanket. "I think I'm *still* dreaming."

She pinches my nipple.

"Ouch! You're supposed to do that to yourself when you're the one unsure of reality."

She slides her hand under the blanket, and I'm pretty sure she pinches her own nipple next—which makes my cock impossibly harder.

"I guess I'm awake," she says grumpily. "But I feel like I'm still in that dream."

"And that might explain why you're still wrapped around me," I say.

She nods. "Also, this." She closes the distance between our lips and gives me a passionate, hot-as-hell kiss.

"So much for no sex," I mutter under my breath when the kiss is over, and she has her delicate hand wrapped around the shaft of my cock.

"You said 'unless I ask.'" She strokes me up and down. "This is me asking."

And she doesn't have to ask me twice.

I spring into action and do not stop until she comes thrice. As my reward, I shoot my load into her pretty mouth, and she swallows before she says, "I did that purely because it's practical."

Though I feel very languid, I find the energy to ask, "How is swallowing practical?"

"We have no water," she explains. "Easier cleanup."

CHAPTER 23
Kendall

WHEN I WAKE UP, I'm wrapped around Ashton like a slutty Snuggie.

Okay, this seems familiar. Does that mean it wasn't a dream when we had sex for the third time?

I scan my body, particularly my private parts.

Shit. I'm sore enough to believe that yes, we did it again.

Which I guess makes sense. I pinched myself and that hurt, so it must not have been a dream. Then again, he made me come three times, each orgasm more powerful than the last—and I swallowed, all of which have never happened outside of a dream before.

I carefully extricate myself and look out the window.

It's still pitch black out, so my best bet is to go back to sleep.

Except sleep doesn't come, and I'm not sure if that's

because I already got my six hours or because I keep replaying our last conversation in my head.

I mean, did Ashton *really* expect me to believe that bullshit about not sleeping with anyone for three years? The very years he got rich and therefore had even more women throwing themselves at him? I mean, he was already swimming in pussy as a trainer at the time we met.

But what if, somehow, he told me the truth?

No, that's impossible.

Then again, it happens. I mean, I'm not hideous or anything, but despite what Emma and my other friends believe, I'm not getting laid on the regular. In fact, in my case, I did have a three-year break from sex—but not because Ashton's big cock ruined me for anyone else or any such nonsense. I've just had bad luck, that's all. Horrible date on top of horrible date.

Could he have been too busy with his business? Or had a streak of bad luck, like I did?

No. No way. Once a dog, always a dog.

Then again, why does it matter to me? Even if he told me the truth, and even if I wanted something more between us, there's a problem.

There's the thing he said about sex workers.

I sneak a worried glance at still-peacefully sleeping Ashton. It's crazy, I know, but even thinking about this so close to him makes me nervous, as if he might somehow overhear my thoughts.

No, that's silly. He's out like a light. And my thoughts are safe inside my head.

I sigh softly.

Something that I don't like to even think about, let alone share with anyone, is that I have a side gig that some—maybe many—would consider… sex work. Not the traditional version, obviously, given my three-year abstinence streak, but there is something I do that's vaguely in the same-ish ballpark.

Unless it's not?

Not for the first time, I wish I'd spoken to Emma or some other friend about my secret project. I didn't do so because I was embarrassed, doubly so because said gig has been the perfect cover for my family's financial troubles.

I *could* talk to Emma after she comes back from her honeymoon.

Nah. Not worth it. In some not-too-distant future, I will come up with my own designs and drop the side gig because I'll have enough money to live on from the job of my dreams.

Speaking of designs, I don't know if it's Ashton's proximity inspiring the idea, but what if I created something like athleisure clothes, but more versatile? I mean, brands like Lululemon make yoga and workout clothes that you can wear to the supermarket, but is it possible to take that a step further and create an outfit that you can wear to the gym, and to work, and even to happy hour afterward?

Maybe even something you can wear to a formal party?

If nothing else, that sounds like a fun challenge.

Yeah, the gears are already turning. It would have to be some kind of a jumpsuit. Hmm. Maybe made out of a stretchy and moisture-wicking material? A blend of nylon and spandex?

Yes. That could work. I'd have to find the perfect ratio.

It would also need breathable lining and a built-in bra.

I can almost see it.

Adjustable straps, of course.

A zipper that's easy to hide.

High-waisted, with tapered legs, so you can wear it equally well with sneakers or heels.

I'd call it FlexiChic.

No. That sounds like a porn site for people with a gymnast fetish.

Maybe VersaWear?

A blood-curdling scream rings out from outside, and my first thought is that Bubba and Dottie have come back, and now he's murdering her with a dull butter knife.

Ashton sits up. "What the fuck?"

Dottie screams again.

Ashton leaps to his feet and rushes outside.

"Wait!"

I reluctantly follow him, cursing testosterone as I go. I mean, who runs *toward* such a scream?

Once I'm out, I find Ashton sans Dottie or Bubba, and cursing very creatively in the faint light from the half-moon above.

A moment later, I hear one more "scream."

No, not a scream.

It's a call of a large bird that resembles a crane. And now that I see the source, the call sounds much less like a woman being brutally tortured via butter knife and more like a "kwee." Which is a good thing.

"That's a limpkin," Ashton says.

"A limp what?"

"Limpkin," he enunciates. "I saw one on the way here, but it was blissfully silent. Bubba did tell me they have 'interesting' calls."

I grimace. "Leave it to that guy to redefine 'horrifying' as 'interesting.' By that logic, this tour is very interesting."

Ashton frowns. "I can't believe they're not back. It's almost dawn. We were supposed to see the bioluminescence together—which implies evening or nighttime."

My reply is my best "I told you so" look. "If they drowned during the storm, we're screwed," I say. "Even if our friends look for us, I'm not sure they'll be able to find us. After all, Bubba kept emphasizing how secret this place is. What if it's not on any maps? What if—"

"Let's not spiral," Ashton says, a bit grimly. "When it gets light out, I'll take a look at that boat once again. Maybe they left the key somewhere inside, or nearby?"

"It's possible." I heroically resist reminding him about his skepticism over our ability to find our way out on a boat.

He gestures for me to go back inside.

"No, you go ahead," I tell him. "I'll join in a second."

He frowns. "Oh?"

"Nature calls."

He nods and steps into the cabin.

With a sigh, I brave the outhouse, and by the time I'm done using it, I feel violated and in need of a shower—which isn't available.

When I return to the cabin, Ashton hands me a bottle of hand sanitizer, and I want to kiss him for being so much better prepared—but I don't, obviously, because reasons.

He returns to whatever he was doing by the water cooler.

I walk over and stare as he separates the trail mix into subcomponents.

"What are you doing?" I ask.

"Breakfast."

"Yeah. Okay. That explains everything."

"I figured I'd make you hot chocolate," he says and gestures at the cup with M&Ms.

My stomach feels fluttery at his thoughtfulness—or maybe I just swallowed a few of the fireflies while I was asleep.

"How?" I ask.

"First, I will crush them in a plastic bag. Next, I will melt the powder over that"—he gestures at the candle —"and combine it with water."

"Wow." I take the cup with the chocolates. "How about I save you the trouble? I'm happy to eat them as is and then chase them down with water."

"Sure, I guess," he says, then takes the assortment of dried fruit he had separated and dunks them into a glass with water.

"What's that about?" I ask.

He shrugs. "It makes them taste more like real fruit?"

Is that a good thing? But more importantly... "Why are you separating the peanuts?"

Another shrug. "They're my favorite, so I wanted to enjoy a handful all at once."

Huh. "I like walnuts myself."

He gestures at the cup that contains nuts and seeds that aren't peanuts. "Help yourself."

We proceed to harvest our breakfast from there, which is a lot more enjoyable than you'd expect. I even like the rehydrated dried fruit—especially because it doesn't stick to your teeth like the regular version. Not to mention, the leftover water from said fruit is a delicacy in itself.

As we eat and drink, Ashton tells me what else he's considered making from the trail mix: ideas that include things like porridge, nut cheese, and protein bars.

"If only we had a blender," he says wistfully. "I'd make a killer smoothie with what we have."

I sip the dry-fruit emulsion water. "Looks like you have a backup career option as a chef."

He smiles. "I give people advice on what to eat, and they often say, 'But that won't taste good,' so I have to be ready with recipe ideas that contradict such statements." He looks thoughtful for a second. "You know, maybe that should be the next feature of ThriveFit."

"Food?"

He shakes his head. "We can already track calories and nutrition, but we don't offer recipes. It might be nice if you could give ThriveFit healthy ingredients, and it suggested what you could make... It might require AI or something like that. I'll have to talk to my sister about this."

Huh. Who knew that watching a man come up with improvements to software could be such a turn-on?

"My brother works with AI," I tell him. "Maybe I could put you in touch?"

Assuming we leave this swamp alive.

Ashton's eyes light up. "That would be amazing, thanks."

"It's no big deal." Cameron will be happy to get more business for his company.

"So, what about you?" Ashton asks. "Do *you* have a backup career?"

"No." But if I were crazy enough to tell him about my secret source of income, this would be a great time. "It's fashion or nothing."

He nods. "That's being focused. It should only help."

"I'm not sure I'm focused enough," I say. "Tierre has got me so busy at work that I haven't had the time to sit down and come up with my own ideas."

Ashton sweeps a hand over the dingy room. "Take advantage of the enforced downtime."

"I already have," I admit, and then tell him about my VersaWear idea.

"That sounds great," he says. "I have countless clients who'd find such a thing useful. In fact, when it's finished, I'd be glad to plug VersaWear for you."

Seriously, how many of those damned fireflies did I swallow?

"That's too generous," I say. "I'm not sure I can accept."

He waves that off. "Let's make a deal. When you're done, let me check it out. If it's as good as it sounds, it would actually help my business to promote it."

"It would?" Sounds too good to be true.

"Whenever I make my clients happy, especially the celebs, it obviously helps my business."

"I guess... Well, if I make my VersaWear design a reality, you'll be the first person I ping." After I unblock his number, that is.

"Perfect." He nods toward the window. "Now, how about we celebrate our pact by watching the sunrise together?"

"Sure." Though it sounds a bit too romantic for my sanity.

As we leave the cabin and head toward the water, the sun just starts to peek over the horizon.

"From where should we watch it?" I ask.

"The boat has seats," he says. "Let's watch from there, and once everything is sufficiently illuminated, we can look for keys."

"That works." I have no idea why I do this, but I

grab his hand—and am rewarded with the predictable sensual zings that always accompany his touch.

Squeezing my hand tenderly, he walks me to the boat, where we take our seats side by side, our knees touching.

Trying to ignore the impact of his nearness, I watch the majestic way the sun paints the sky in pink, orange, and gold hues. "This reminds me of some paintings we studied in my Art and Design History course."

"Oh, yeah? Which ones?"

He likes art too? "'Impression, Sunrise' by Monet. But also 'Forest Sunrise' by Albert Bierstadt."

He nods thoughtfully. "I've only seen the Monet, and you're spot on. I'll need to check out the other one when we get back to civilization."

I don't counter with "*if* we get back to civilization" because the moment is too pleasant to spoil with such thoughts, no matter how pragmatic. I'm not surprised he's familiar with that painting. A family like the Vancrofts probably travel regularly to Paris, so he could've seen the original in the Marmottan Monet Museum.

As the sunrise continues, we take turns noticing details that create the ethereal, and way-too-romantic, atmosphere—like the mist that hovers softly over the swamp and the herons walking bravely up to a gator, who in turn looks like he's also enjoying the sunrise.

Once the sun is finally up, Ashton and I turn toward each other at the same exact time, and our lips come together as if of their own accord.

This kiss is sweet and tender, and it does to my lips what the sunrise has done for my eyes.

When things start to heat up, I force myself to pull away.

"We should look for those keys," I say, more than a little breathlessly.

"Ah. Right." He stands up. "Let's."

We scour the boat and then the surrounding area, literally leaving no stone unturned.

Sadly, all we have to show for our troubles is a rusty hammer that Ashton finds in the small console storage space.

He, however, looks extremely pleased with his find.

"Something to bash Bubba over the head with?" I ask, only half-jokingly.

"No," he says. "I was thinking this will make it easier to crush nuts if I want to make a porridge, and—though I'm not sure it will work—smash peanuts into peanut butter."

I sigh. "I see you're now as convinced as I am that we're stuck here for a while."

"Just want to be prepared. And to that end..." He motions toward something on the ground. "This place is littered with apple snails—and we have the water to boil them, if you're interested."

I stare at him, but he's clearly serious. "No. Not desperate enough for that yet."

He scoffs. "Why? You've never had escargot?"

I scoff right back. "I'm not grossed out by snails, if that's what you're talking about." Though frogs, whose legs are another French delicacy, are a different story. "I gladly eat escargot, and I use snail mucin on my face."

He wrinkles his nose at that last one. "What's the problem then?"

"According to the waiver that *both of us* signed, the local snails carry rat lungworm," I remind him pointedly.

"Right," he says. "Which is why we'd boil them."

"And you're sure rat lungworm is not some sort of an extremophile germ that can survive a boiling?"

He purses his lips. "I'm pretty sure, but you have a point. We'll wait until we're really desperate."

Fuck. "Maybe we should go back to you being the optimistic one. When you talk like that, I get the feeling we're going to die here."

"We won't," he says confidently. "I know a bit about survivalism, and I've given this some thought. There's fish all around us. I can make a spear. Or a bow using the rubber band in my pants. Armed with those, I can try bowfishing or spearfishing—maybe even regular fishing if I manage to make a rod. The bow and spear will also allow me to take down that annoying bird—which I bet tastes like chicken. And if I'm feeling really brave, I can hit a gator on the head with this hammer."

I gape at him. "That's a lot of plans. Are you planning for us to grow old here, Robinson Crusoe style?"

Except with a lot more sex. Friday and Robinson Crusoe didn't have sex, right? Relatedly, did Tom

Hanks face-fuck the volleyball, Wilson, in *Cast Away*? He did draw a mouth on it, after all. I'll need to look into this when—or if—I get access to the internet again.

Ashton smiles. "We'll get out of here shortly. I just thought that coming up with multiple means of survival would calm you."

"But don't we still have a water problem?" I can't help but ask. And I don't mean just drinking it. If I don't shower for two days, I may just die from griminess.

He gestures at the swamp. "We can boil that water if super desperate. But a better option might be to collect the rain water next time—and then boil that, just in case. If we're still here when we finish the first water cooler bottle, we can put it outside and rig up a funnel into it to collect maximum water."

Note to self: if it rains again, use that water to shower.

"Interesting." Tension I didn't even realize I had leaves my body. "I guess we really *will* survive."

"And thrive—if we have to. Now, I was thinking we should take our phones and walk all over this island to see if we can get a signal."

This is the best idea anyone has had since the invention of the vibrator, so I jump on it with enthusiasm. Sadly, we fail to locate any signal—even when Ashton climbs onto the roof of his cabin.

"Be careful," I say sternly as he climbs down.

He chuckles. "I'm touched that you care."

"If you break your leg, who will be spearfishing?" I grumble. "Or MacGyvering us a toaster out of a... toad."

He looks thoughtful as he gets all the way down. "I know you were just kidding, but you just gave me an idea."

I narrow my eyes. "I'm not eating toads. I'll starve first. Or eat you."

He laughs. "That's not it. I just remembered that we're in the Sunshine State, which means a solar cooker would be pretty practical."

"A what?"

"It's like a DIY oven," he explains. "I think I can make one if I rip off some of that reflective material from the boat."

"And it will cook?"

He nods. "In the heat, the temperature can reach three hundred degrees."

"It's official," I say. "If we survive this, but there's a zombie apocalypse after, I want to be with you."

I expect him to make a "repopulate the Earth" joke, but he looks worriedly at the sun instead.

"We should hide," he says. "Before we get overheated."

We get into the cabin, and Ashton starts gathering our clothes.

"I'm going to hang them to dry," he explains.

I nod.

He does as he said, then comes back and pours us each a glass of water.

"So… what now?" I ask.

He shrugs. "Usually I'd exercise, but I'm not sure it's a good idea given the limited food and water situation, not to mention the lack of shower."

Counterpoint: his exercising would have a lot of entertainment value for me. But I decide against telling him that.

"I guess we can just hang out and talk," I say.

"Sure." He takes a seat at the table. "What kind of music do you like?"

"To play or listen to?" I blurt, and instantly regret it.

"Play?" His eyebrow turns into a question mark.

With a sigh, I take a seat. "My instrument is the sousaphone. Or it was, at least. And my favorite piece that features it is *The Muppet Show* theme."

I silently dare him to make jokes about me blowing. I heard them all back in high school.

Ashton cocks his head. "The sousaphone is like a tuba, right? One that wraps around your body?" For some unfathomable reason, he examines me with heat in his eyes.

"You can't walk with a tuba," I say. "And it would sound like crap outside."

Shit. Ashton's eyes light up as he connects the dots. "You were in the marching band?"

"You get great exercise from it," I say defensively. "Something someone like you should appreciate. Plus, it looked great on my college application."

"Hey, I have nothing against it. I bet you looked cute in your band uniform."

"I was underaged at the time, you perv." But I do appreciate how little he's teased me so far—even less than Emma did when I shared this with her. "Now you owe me something embarrassing about yourself."

"Being in a marching band isn't embarrassing," he says.

"Chicken."

"Fine." He grins. "A few years back, I went to check out puppy yoga at the gym where I was working. I got there early, so it was just me and the pups. Oh—and something I should mention about myself is that I like to talk to dogs. So, anyway, I was so absorbed in my conversation that I didn't notice as the whole group and the yoga teacher gathered behind me. When I saw them—"

"They started to ovulate?" I interject.

"Why?"

"Because that sounds more adorable than embarrassing." And I bet he slept with every female in that class as a result.

"I wasn't done with the story," he says. "When the class started, for whatever reason, a German shepherd puppy named Waggatha Christie kept sniffing my butt."

"Oh, please. That barely passes as an embarrassing story." I'd bet good money all the other bitches in that class wanted to sniff around him. Waggatha Christie just had the chutzpah.

"You never said what music you like to listen to," he says, deftly changing the subject.

"The Four Seasons," I say. "By Vivaldi."

"No way." He takes out his phone. "Check this out." He taps his screen a few times, and the familiar sounds of violins ring out from the tiny speakers.

"That's *my* favorite piece of music," he explains. "So much so that I downloaded it in case I want to listen to it while I'm stuck somewhere without service."

For the next few minutes, we sit in a companiable silence, enjoying the music.

"So," he says when the Spring part of the concerti concludes, and Summer begins. "Tell me more about yourself."

"Like what?"

"Surprise me."

I shrug. "I have a single bar stool in my apartment."

"Why only one?" he asks.

"No space for more, and after dealing with my infuriating boss all day, I like to get home and relax with a glass of wine."

He chuckles. "That almost makes sense."

"What about you?"

He smirks. "I have a traffic cone in my closet."

"You do?"

He nods. "When I foster boy pups that need to learn how to go on a wee-wee pad, I put the cone on said pad to help them out."

"That also *almost* makes sense."

We continue sharing random factoids about ourselves for a while, though some turn out to be controversial, like the fact that I jaywalk.

"You could get run over," he says sternly. "In trying to save a minute by not walking to the crosswalk, you could delay yourself for days or longer, if you end up in the hospital—or worse."

I reply with an eyeroll, and we continue the back and forth, which more and more reminds me of a get-to-know-you part of a good date.

"Mind if I take my shirt off?" Ashton asks just as I have my epiphany. "It's getting hotter."

It *is* getting hotter, and in more ways than one.

"Why would I mind?" I reply.

Given the kind of body Ashton possesses, I mind when it's hidden.

"Cool." He takes his shirt off.

Hmm.

If I didn't want this to seem more like a date—or specifically, what happens at the conclusion of a third one—I should've objected, after all. Seeing the lickable beads of sweat glistening on his muscles makes my mouth—and other parts—water.

"It *is* hot in here," I say huskily. "Mind if I—"

"Hold that thought," he says and hurries out of the cabin.

Huh?

When he comes back, I understand why.

He's brought back my bra and panties, which have already dried in the heat of the sun.

"You've already seen all my bits," I remind him. "Why would you want me to hide them now?"

His nostrils flare. "I'm not sure I'd be able to carry

on a conversation if you were naked in front of me. Seeing you in that slip has been painful enough."

"Oh?" I teasingly tug at the strap of my slip. "You might want to turn around."

He nearly gives himself whiplash as he turns.

Feeling much sexier than our lack of civilization should allow, I put on my underwear before I tell him he can turn back.

When he does, he scans me hungrily, and his jaw ticks. "I was wrong. This might actually make the situation worse than if you *were* naked."

I moisten my lips. "It's not like I had a lot more to say anyway."

He throws a meaningful glance at the bed. "There are ways to get to know each other that don't involve words."

I reach over and feel his perfect cock through his pants. "In that case, I'd like you to get to know me *a lot* better."

CHAPTER 24

Ashton

"THAT WAS HOT," Kendall says as she's lying in my arms after I give her three more "get to know each other" orgasms.

"Let's not use the h-word," I say, feeling on the verge of panting like a dog. "Also banned are: balmy, boiling, scorching, and sweltering."

With a laugh, she jumps off the bed, still gloriously naked, and pours each of us a glass of water.

I drain my glass in one gulp. "I think we should hang our clothes to block the windows." I point at the one that the sun shines through. "Especially that one."

She agrees, so I fetch the dried clothes and use them as curtains with the help of the hammer I found and a few nails I salvage from the floorboards.

"I feel cooler already," Kendall says sarcastically. "Now what?"

I rub my stomach. "Lunch?" We need plenty of electrolytes given our situation.

"What do you have in mind? Porridge?"

I shake my head. "I don't think I'll ever want to eat something warm again." Except maybe her sweet pussy, of course. "I'm thinking of munching on nuts and resoaked fruit. What about you?"

"Same," she says. "But with some M&Ms for dessert."

We spend some time separating the trail mix once more while chatting about our lives in New York. After we've managed to fill an entire glass with M&Ms, Kendall eyes them and wonders out loud why they aren't melting.

"Great question," I say. "Probably because despite how it feels, it's not yet as hot in here as it would be in your mouth." And her mouth is the hottest place on the planet, or at least the hottest place I've had my cock visit.

"Hmm," she says. "Why do they melt in your mouth but not in your hand?"

I shrug. "Hands are colder?"

"Not by that much," she says. "I suspect the coating must have something to do with it. When I hold regular chocolate, especially the cheap milk kind, it does melt in my hands."

"I guess we'll know we're in trouble if this stuff starts to melt," I tell her. "Hydrate extra if it happens."

"So... what do we do now?" she asks.

"Rock, paper, scissors?" I suggest, and my cock twitches.

He clearly has a better idea of what to do, even if it's not original.

"Prepare to be massacred." Kendall forms a tight fist. "I'm so good at this game I could get paid for it."

I also make a fist. "Would you also say that you'd 'make money hand over fist?'"

She groans. "One, two, three."

She throws paper, and I throw rock.

"See?" she says.

"Beginner's luck. Let's go again."

She grins mischievously. "Care to make this more interesting?"

I gesture at my naked torso. "Before you say *strip* rock, paper, scissors, remember that we don't have much on."

"I was actually going to suggest that the loser do a service for the winner," she says. "It can be sexual but doesn't have to be."

"Deal." Someone needs to give me some paper to help with the rock that my cock has just turned into. "What favor do you want if you win?"

She looks thoughtful. "A massage. And you?"

"Oh, you don't need to beat me for that. I'd be happy to oblige."

"You didn't think this through," she says. "I'll be naked, and you'll get very horny—but I want the massage to last for an hour, and for you to use both hands, meaning you can't jerk off or anything like that the whole time."

Oh. "You drive a *hard* bargain. I'll just have to make sure not to lose."

She moistens her lips. "And what do you want on the off chance you manage to win?"

"Also a massage. But in my version, you *can't* use your hands."

"How then?"

"You can slide your breasts down my back, or use your feet, or—"

"Got it," she says. "Obviously, that's purely hypothetical as I don't plan to lose."

"Me neither."

"On three," she says and counts it down.

She throws rock, and I throw scissors.

"Loser," she taunts. "Come, service me."

She sashays over to the bed, takes off her bra and panties, and sprawls there, her shapely ass in the air. "Remember, you owe me an hour."

"Fine." I play "The Four Seasons" on my phone again to help her relax before walking over to the bed, at which point I have to fight the urge to take her from behind, hard.

"Here goes." My hand touches her warm skin, and my dick wants to howl at the moon.

"Yes," she murmurs as I knead her shoulders. "Just like that."

How is it that I'm going this crazy for her? It's not for lack of sex. In fact, the last time I came as much as I have in the past twenty-four hours was when I discovered jerking off as a teen.

But a deal is a deal, so I continue, though not touching myself is a form of torture that goes against the Geneva Convention.

Kendall moans in pleasure.

Fuck me. "Seriously? Are you really enjoying yourself that much, or are you just messing with me?"

"You're that good," she says languidly. "And it's official: your backup career shouldn't be as a chef. You're a born masseuse."

I move on to her lower back, and her moans intensify—and so does my sexual torment. Things only get worse when I massage her glutes, for obvious reasons, and they don't improve when I move down to her long legs.

"Can you do my feet?" she murmurs when I get to her calves.

Fuuuck. Am I developing a foot fetish? Holding her perfect feet has a more engorging effect on me than her ass did—though I guess it's all cumulative.

"Okay," she says finally. "I'm ready to turn over."

She flips over, and I can't help but notice that her nipples are pebbled, which can't be because she's cold.

"Continue," she commands.

With a barely suppressed groan, I do, but I make my touches more sensual than therapeutic, working on her neck and ears first, then her scalp and inner wrists.

Her moans turn more carnal, and her nipples morph into tiny rocks, proving I'm on the right track.

"I'm going to work on your lower abdominals," I say hoarsely and slide my hands down her body, past her deliciously round breasts and her delectable navel, stopping just short of her pubic bone.

"Ashton," she says after I massage the area for about a minute. Her eyes are heavy-lidded. "Can I have a happy ending?"

My cock hardens even more, and it's all I can do not to growl as I say, "Of course."

"On second thought, I think I might be too sore for that." She gestures at said appendage.

Which is now a sad appendage.

"How about I give your clit a little massage?" I suggest gruffly. "With my tongue."

Her pupils dilate, but she looks uncertain.

"Let me try it," I whisper. "And if you're too sore, just let me know."

She nods minutely.

I slowly retrace the path my hands just took with my tongue, until I reach her pink little pussy and give her clit a featherlight kiss.

"Wow," she breathes.

"I'm just getting started." I make a teasing circle around her clit.

She arches her back.

I smirk and give the swollen nub a tiny lick.

Kendall moans, so my next lick is firmer, as is the one after that.

"Oh, my," she gasps as I flatten my tongue against my target. "I'm going to come."

"Yes," I rasp right into her clit. "Come for me, now."

And boy, does she. Arching off the bed, she orgasms with a wild, almost desperate cry.

I embrace her as she recovers.

"Sorry about that screech at the end," she says, hiding her face against my shoulder.

Though my balls are desperately blue, I can't help but grin. "I took it as a compliment."

She snorts. "I bet I sounded like a horny limpkin bird."

Hearing the word "horny," my swollen cock decides to join the conversation by twitching, and as a result, poking Kendall in her thigh.

She looks between our bodies. "You know, despite how terrible you are at rock, paper, scissors, you've earned yourself a reward."

"Oh?"

"Get on your stomach," she says. "I'll give you that no-hands massage… to start."

I do as she says, though I wish there were a hole in this bed big enough to stick my dick into, as it's so hard I'm uncomfortable.

"How's this?" She glides her breasts down my back.

"Fucking amazing," I grunt back.

"And this?" She drags her tongue down my spine before gliding her whole body down the same path.

"I have no words," I mutter, and I really don't. There's too little blood going to my brain.

"Let's try this." She stands on the bed, and I feel her feet taking turns massaging my shoulders and then my glutes.

"Fuck. That feels amazing. Better than any massage I've ever gotten." Hotter too. "Just be careful not to fall."

She scoffs and massages my lower back with her feet until I think I might just burst.

Then she sits back on the bed. "Ready to turn around?"

I rotate with a speed that would put to shame a blade in the turbine of a fighter jet.

She sits at the end of the bed, cups her breasts seductively, and reaches her feet toward my aching cock—leaving her pussy splayed open for my hungry gaze.

"Are you ready for *your* happy ending?" she asks, her voice the very definition of sultry.

I grunt something unintelligible before her feet encircle my aching erection, then slide up and down.

A groan of pleasure escapes my lips.

"Kendall," I growl. "I don't think I can last long."

"Good." She glides her feet up and down again, and I come all over her pretty toes.

CHAPTER 25

Kendall

IF GETTING STRANDED with Ashton seemed like a date in the beginning, it's now starting to feel like a honeymoon, especially as I lie in his embrace, enjoying another post-orgasmic haze.

Ashton's stomach rumbles. "Want to have dinner?" he asks lazily.

I do, so we munch on the trail mix and talk, getting to know each other even better—which is probably a bad idea, but I just can't help myself. Despite the messiness of whatever this is between us and my conflicting feelings, I'm hungry for every detail about him, no matter how trivial.

I think the reverse is true as well because he doesn't stop peppering me with questions. By now, he may know more about me than all of my previous boyfriends combined—not that I'm saying he's my boyfriend, of course.

"Want to play 'Two Truths and a Lie?'" Ashton asks after we finish eating.

"Is that to spruce up the 'get-to-know-you?'"

He shrugs. "What else is there to do?"

"All right. Want to go first?"

He shakes his head. "You go. I'm very good at this game, so you need all the help you can get."

How is going first going to help me? Also… "Should we do random facts or have a theme?"

His eyes heat up. "How about we make it dirty?"

"Huh." I think for a couple of seconds. "I haven't had sex for three years. I once showed up on a date wearing an anal plug. I liked giving you that foot job."

Ashton's nostrils flare. "The anal plug?"

"Damn it," I say.

"But… three years?" he says. "Are you some sort of camel when it comes to orgasms? Got enough that one night with me?"

"Please." I scoff. "I simply haven't been dating much. Because of too much work and bad luck. It had zero to do with you."

"Sure. Sure."

"Your turn," I say grumpily.

He purses his lips. "Your pussy tastes like apples. Your nipples taste like hibiscus. And your mouth tastes like vanilla."

Hmm. "They all sound like lies."

"Does that mean you give up?"

"No. I think the nipple thing is a lie."

"Nope," he says. "Your mouth doesn't taste like vanilla."

I know he wants me to ask what it *does* taste like, so I don't give him the satisfaction. "That was cheating," I say instead. "My pussy doesn't taste like apples."

"Oh." He walks up to me and licks his finger. "Care to put that to the test?"

If I weren't so sore, I'd be dying to have those fingers inside me. Even as is, the proposition is too tempting.

"I've tasted myself before." Granted, it's been a while. "I didn't taste any apples." Then again, I do like those apple strudels they sell at the bakery near my house. And I've been drinking plenty of fresh-squeezed juice made from apples and carrots, so if you are what you eat...

"Does anything of mine taste like a carrot?" I ask.

He shakes his head, grinning. "But hey, taste is a very subjective experience."

I roll my eyes. "I think I want to play something else."

"Sore loser much?"

Loser, no. Sore—very much so.

"How about a round of 'would you rather?'" I suggest.

He agrees, and we play that for a while. Among other things, I learn that Ashton would rather explore the deep sea than go into space, and he learns that if a time machine existed, I'd rather meet my ancestors than my descendants.

"Is it getting cooler, or is it just me?" Ashton asks after I admit that I'd rather speak like Yoda than breathe like Darth Vader.

"Yeah." I walk up to the window and raise the makeshift curtains. "I think the sun is setting."

Ashton leaps to his feet. "Want to go for a stroll?"

"Sure. We can play 'I spy' as we do."

I ENJOY CIRCLING THE ISLAND A LOT, AND AS IT TURNS out, I'm much better than Ashton at "I spy."

"My turn," he says after it takes him five questions to zero in on the cypress tree. "I spy with my little eye something small."

I grin. "So… not your cock?"

He chuckles. "Unlike my cock, this thing can fly."

"Don't sell your cock short. It made me feel like I could fly."

"This thing can buzz too."

I grin. "So… a tiny vibrator?"

He looks around. "How would I spy *that*?"

"Sheesh, touchy. You're obviously talking about a mosquito."

"Finally." He slaps his forearm. "I think now that the sun is setting, they're out for a meal."

I wrinkle my nose. "Let's hide."

He points to the cabin nearer the water. "Want to see if your bed is now usable?"

Shit. It probably is. I can see that the water has receded, and we left the door open, so the smell must have cleared out. The problem is, I don't like the idea of not sharing a bed anymore. If we ever get off this island, then sure. But as is...

"You're not going to kick me out of yours so easily," I say. "But if you want to go to that cabin yourself and—"

"Nope. You're not going to kick me out of 'mine' either."

We hide out for a couple of hours, then come out when it's completely dark and the mosquitoes are less active. However, the temperature has dropped so much that we have to return, remove our clothes from the window, and put them all on.

Even with the extra layers, we only stay out for an hour to enjoy the light display before we get back into the cabin and jump into bed in a spooning position to warm up.

"That was a nice day," I muse. "Considering."

"I enjoyed it too," he murmurs into the crook of my neck. "Considering."

Feeling obscenely cozy in his arms, I close my eyes and immediately pass out.

I WAKE WITH A START.

Someone is banging on the door.

"Stay back," Ashton tells me, then goes over to open it.

It's Bubba, looking disheveled, and Dottie, looking frightened by the expression she must see on Ashton's face.

"*You*," Ashton growls.

With the lethal speed of a predator, he pounces—and has Bubba dangling in the air in a millisecond.

"Where the fuck were you?" The question is accompanied by a rough shake.

"Oi, don't hurt Bubbala!" Dottie shouts. "Our boat broke. We forked out extra to get it sorted ASAP."

Ashton drops the tour guide. "Why didn't you leave us the keys to the other boat?"

"Oh," Dottie says. "We didn't reckon you'd be needing it, mate."

"Take us back, now," Ashton orders through gritted teeth.

"And pray I don't feel litigious when I get home," I add, matching his tone.

Looking sullen, the tour guides help us get into their boats. After a short argument, it's decided that I will go with Bubba and Ashton with Dottie—because no one is sure if Bubba would survive the trip otherwise.

Possibly murderous inclinations aside, I must admit that I find pissed-off Ashton *very* hot. He is magnificent in his fury—a fury he hid pretty well until the last second, by the way.

"Now, listen to me carefully," Ashton says to Bubba, enunciating each word with cool precision. "You can ride with Kendall, but if she arrives at the shore with so much as a hair out of place, I will make you *very* sorry, and no excuses will save you."

Looking like he's on the verge of peeing his pants, Bubba nods profusely and mutters, "Yes, sir. Of course, sir."

"Ashton had better get to our destination in one piece also," I say to Dottie. "Or else."

I have no idea what "or else" implies in my case, but my ride with Bubba happens in a sullen silence—at least until we get close enough to civilization for my cell service to show up again. As soon I get a couple of bars, a million messages flood my phone, the majority from my mom, Emma, and Mr. Boss, along with a few from my brother.

I call Mom first, and explaining takes a while, especially when she hears there was a guy involved. The only reason I mention Ashton is because I know that it will make her retroactively feel better about the whole situation. For whatever reason, Mom doesn't think a woman can survive without a man, especially in the wilderness.

"What's his name?" Mom asks when I'm done.

Leave it to Mom to zero in on the trickiest part of the tale.

"Ashton," I say. "He was a groomsman at the wedding."

"Oh," she says, imbuing the word with all sorts of meaning that one doesn't want to discuss with a parent. "Is he cute?"

"I have to call more people now."

"Please thank Ashton for me," Mom says. "And tell him your father and I want to buy him dinner."

Yeah. No. "Gotta go."

I hang up and call Emma to get her up to speed. With her, I skip the part about Ashton's involvement. If she were to tell me that Marcus is searching for Ashton, I'd fess up, but men being men, Marcus probably hasn't noticed his friend has been radio silent for the past two days.

"What about your flight?" she asks.

I sigh. "Missed it. Will have to figure something out."

"That sucks. And I don't think Marcus's plane is—"

"Don't even," I say. "You're on your honeymoon. Just relax."

"Okay…"

"How is that going?" I ask, smiling into the phone.

"Amazing. Fiji has the most beautiful beaches I've ever seen, and the resort is out of this world."

I grin mischievously. "Shouldn't you be singing praises to Marcus's cock?"

Bubba darts me a glance but says nothing—clearly still impressed by his "conversation" with Ashton.

"I was trying to keep my reply appropriate for the spa, which is where I am," Emma says, and I can almost see her pale face turning pink.

"Say no more. I've got to go anyway. You'll tell me all the juicy deets some other time."

Before she can protest, I hang up and call Cameron.

"Hey, sis," he says. "Mom told me you've been located. What happened?"

I give him a brief version of the story without mentioning Ashton.

"Very interesting," Cameron says when I finish. "Anything else you want to share?"

Crap. "Such as?"

He chuckles. "All Mom talked about was your new boyfriend."

"Is that right?" I squeeze the phone tighter.

"Oh, yeah," Cameron says, and I can just see him smirking in that infuriating way of his. "About how he saved you and all that. Odd that you didn't mention him at all."

"Ashton is not my boyfriend," I say, and see Bubba raise his bushy eyebrow. He clearly also has an opinion on this.

"Who is he then?" Cameron asks.

"Emma's new husband's friend," I reply.

"Ah," Cameron says. "You don't want to jeopardize your relationship with your best friend by dating someone close to her husband. I get it."

"*You* get it? The man who cost me two friends because he couldn't resist dating them?" It's actually two friends and one frenemy, but I was glad to be rid of the latter.

He sighs. "Come on, sis. Can't you let that go? It was high school. I didn't do much thinking with my brain."

"Gross." I take a calming breath. "But fine."

No reason to beat this dead horse anymore. After the third incident, Cameron and I got into a big fight, which we resolved by making a pact not to date anyone in our respective circles—a pact he's honored to the best of my knowledge. Then again, I never introduced him to Emma, Janie, or anyone else I was friends with in college, so it's not like he's had an opportunity to betray said pact.

"Anyway," Cameron says. "If you're not dating this guy, how did you get stuck together?"

"Because he took the same cursed tour as I did by sheer accident." I glance at Bubba in time to see him wince. "We collaborated in order to survive. Nothing more."

"So... Mom was right? This guy saved you?"

"We weren't stuck long enough for me to need saving," I say. "But I guess if we had been, he does know an obscene amount about surviving in the wild."

"I see," Cameron says. "How about this? Once you guys are far enough along in your relationship to be meeting each other's families, I'll buy him a drink."

"There is no relationship." Nor can there be one, given Ashton's attitude toward something I'm not ever going to discuss with my brother. "But you probably *should* meet him, sooner rather than later. He wants to add AI features to his app."

"Oh. What app is that?"

"ThriveFit."

"Shit," Cameron says after a moment of silence. "I just looked him up. An amazing catch for you—and a great business opportunity for me. Invite him to my birthday."

"He's not my catch." Also, crap. With everything

that has happened, I almost forgot about my brother's big day. Speaking of… "Do you really want to talk business on your birthday?"

Cameron scoffs. "Are you really going to accuse me of being a workaholic… on my birthday?"

"Today is not your birthday, so I can call you whatever I want."

He sighs. "I agreed to the big shindig for Mom. She guilted me with the story of my birth and how she labored to push me out for twenty-five hours." I can visualize his grimace on the other end of the phone. "If something productive comes out of it, that would make me happy… on my birthday."

Fuck. I can't say no to him now. Except… "I don't know if he'll go to such a family event." I would surely hesitate if our roles were reversed.

"It won't hurt to ask."

"No. I guess not." And if Ashton is insane enough to agree, Mom and Dad could thank him at that time instead of having a separate dinner—which sounds a lot more embarrassing.

"All right," Cameron says. "I've got to run."

"See?" I tell him. "Workaholic."

My brother mumbles something like "incorrigible" as he hangs up the phone.

All right. Time for the most unpleasant part.

I skim the million texts from Tierre.

At first, he was merely annoyed that I was late for work. Once it became clear that I wasn't coming in, he grew increasingly irritated, with texts like, "It was bad enough you took a four-day vacation, but how dare you skip day five?" His last text informs me that I'm fired.

Seriously? No "what happened?" No "Are you okay?"

I check his voicemails, and they follow the same pattern as the texts.

Gritting my teeth, I call the asshole.

"You've got some nerve," Tierre says instead of a hello. "First, you disappear off the face of the Earth, and now you call me like nothing is the matter."

What was I supposed to do? He hasn't even given me a chance to speak yet.

"I had a good reason for my absence," I say as politely as I can. "I went on a tour and—"

"Spare me," Tierre says. "I meant it. You no longer work here."

My stomach feels like it's hit an iceberg. I've heard Tierre say "you're fired" to other people in the heat of the moment, but he usually changes his mind and lets the person keep their job.

"I was stuck on a deserted island." I glare at Bubba. "Barely survived. I can bring you proof." Like maybe that waiver I signed before the tour? Or—

"I've already given your job to someone else," Tierre says with zero remorse.

"You what?"

"I'm going to hang up now," he says. "You're sending me too much negative juju."

With that, he disconnects.

I fight the overwhelming urge to toss my phone into the swamp. Instead, I force myself to check on flights. Naturally, there aren't any available because that would mean that something has gone my way. I call the airline directly, and the so-called customer service agent informs me that the money for my earlier ticket is forfeit, and that, just like it states online, there aren't any flights available for tonight.

Damn it. This means I'll need somewhere to stay, and I have no idea if Marcus booked that mansion beyond yesterday.

Speaking of which, what about my stuff at the mansion?

I stress over all of these questions until we reach the shore, where Dottie and Ashton are already waiting.

Ashton must notice my gloomy expression when we get off the boat because he grabs Bubba by his collar, lifts him in the air again, and after a shake, demands, "What did you do?"

"It wasn't him," I say quickly.

"Oh." Ashton sets Bubba back on his feet. "What happened?"

"Not now," I say. "We have bigger problems."

Ashton frowns. "Like?"

"Like our stuff."

He waves my words away. "I called Marcus. The staff at the mansion packed our suitcases. They're waiting for us in the garage."

"Oh. Great. Can we sleep there one more night?"

And if so, would we share a room, as per our new tradition? It's probably a bad idea, but I could—

"Why sleep there?" he asks. "We have a private plane waiting."

Oh. "Must be nice to be so rich."

"I wouldn't know," he says with a grin. "It's Marcus's plane."

"I obviously knew that," I mutter.

He leads me to where a car is already waiting for us, and as we drive to the mansion, I tell him about losing my job.

"That fucker," he says grimly. "But you know what? You're better off."

"Am I?"

He puts a reassuring arm around my shoulders. "If he can fire you like that after three years, and over basically nothing, then fuck him."

"Maybe you're right." And Ashton doesn't even know that my salary from that job wasn't enough to pay my bills. "I've already learned everything I wanted to learn from him."

"There you go. It's time you work for yourself. Create VersaWear, or something else that inspires you."

"Yeah." I feel a jolt of excitement. "That's exactly what I'll do."

"Did you bring your laptop with you on the trip?"

I nod.

"Why don't you work on VersaWear on the flight back? I'll help as much as I can."

How wrong would it be if I jumped on his cock right here and now? The driver wouldn't mind, right?

Before I get the chance to do anything, we pull up to the mansion.

"Can you wait for us?" Ashton asks the driver. "It might be a few minutes, but I'll make it worth your while."

The driver agrees, and we walk up to the mansion, where the butler takes us to our suitcases.

"Can we shower and change before we go?" I ask.

"Sure," the manager says. "No one is using the steam room at the moment. There are showers there and a locker room."

We head over there, and when the warm water hits my skin, I barely suppress a moan of pleasure.

How did humanity survive without showers for the majority of its history?

After the shower, I debate whether to dress comfortably for the flight or to make Ashton want me.

Then again, why choose? I've got a bodysuit and skinny jeans with me. Yeah. But I won't go overboard and wear heels on the plane. Instead, I put on a fresh pair of socks and sneakers, then work on my makeup.

Feeling amazing, especially for someone who's just lost her job, I exit the changing room and smile at Ashton, who's already waiting for me.

The heat in his eyes tells me my outfit is working as intended.

Oh, and boy, did he clean up well also. His face is freshly shaved, his skin glowing, and his lush golden hair would look right at home in a shampoo commercial. To make matters worse—or better—he's wearing a tight white polo shirt, navy fitted chinos, and brown leather boots, a combo that makes me want to strip him naked.

"Should we go?" he asks.

I walk up to him. "Maybe. Or maybe—"

The stupid manager comes in at that very moment and asks if there's anything else we need.

Getting the hint, Ashton gives the guy an obscene tip, and we return to the car with our luggage.

"If you'd like, I can call a few of my clients and consult with them on VersaWear," Ashton says as we get going.

I glance at him. "I'm not sure…"

"Let's give it a shot," he says and calls someone named Megan. He introduces me and asks her what features she'd want in an outfit that can be worn for workouts and out.

"Interesting question," she says, and it finally clicks that this is *the* Megan—who happens to be one of the hottest women in Hollywood.

In a daze, I listen to her ideas—most of them annoyingly good—and then swear to send her a prototype of VersaWear when (not if) it becomes reality.

As soon as we hang up, Ashton calls a few other celebs, and I pick their brains until we get on the plane and take off.

"So," he says. "Ready to work on it now?"

I scan our luxurious—and very private—surroundings. "I think I need to process what Megan and the others have said. And do some market research. And sleep on it."

"Makes sense," Ashton says.

The captain comes on the intercom, informing us that we can unbuckle our safety belts.

"So." I moisten my lips. "We have two hours to kill…"

"Right." Ashton pulls me to him. "I think it's time we joined the Mile High Club."

CHAPTER 26

Ashton

IT'S OFFICIAL. I'm completely and utterly addicted to Kendall—and our in-the-air quickie has only made it worse.

"So..." she says once we put our clothes back on and recline in the super-comfortable chairs. "Did you join the Mile High Club for the first time today, or—"

"Today. You?"

"Same. That is, assuming you're telling the truth."

I cover her hand with mine. "Why would I lie?"

She bites her lip. "To make yourself sound less promiscuous?"

I blow out a breath. "Are we back to that nonsense?"

She shrugs. "I still find it difficult to believe that you had three years of abstinence. Especially with temptations like Megan floating around you at all times."

Fuck. I pull my hand away. "You should trust me."

Isn't that the cornerstone of a serious relationship?

Because that's where I feel we're headed—and to my surprise, I'm not freaked out at all. The opposite, actually.

"You're just suspiciously good at sex," she continues.

"Thanks?" I arch an eyebrow. "So are you."

She rolls her eyes. "By that, I mean the kind of good that takes dedicated practice."

Huh. "When I was in business school, I didn't have time to ride a bike," I point out. "But once I got back on one, the skills came back instantly." Coincidentally, it helped that the bike I got on was a Pinarello masterpiece with outstanding aerodynamic design, lightweight construction, and curvy wheels that—

"I want to believe you," she says but doesn't sound convinced.

I don't know what else to say, but I'm not too concerned. Trust is earned, which means once we're together long enough, it will come naturally. I hope.

"Okay, changing the topic," she says. "I spoke to my brother, and he'd be happy to talk to you about AI."

"Thanks. That's great." I like it that she was talking about me when we weren't together, and to her family on top of that.

She wrinkles her nose. "Don't thank me yet. There's a catch."

"Oh?"

"He wants to talk to you during his birthday party."

"Right, so... what's the catch?"

She snorts. "My whole family will be there."

"And?" I get that we haven't been together that long,

but given how I've been feeling about us, meeting her family doesn't seem too crazy.

Which, of course, *is* crazy—and probably karma at work for making fun of Marcus when things seemed to go too fast between him and Emma.

"Hey, if you don't see a problem, it's all good," Kendall says.

"Can I bring a guest?" I ask.

"Sure. Who?"

"My CTO. In case the conversation gets too technical for me."

"Yeah, sure. I'll let Cameron know."

"When is the event?"

"The day after tomorrow."

"Oh, shit. I need to let my CTO know."

Pulling out my phone, I call Jordan, but she doesn't pick up.

Ah. Right. She told me she was going hiking.

I write her a text, explaining the situation.

When I called Jordan from the boat and told her what happened, she begged to meet my girlfriend as soon as humanly possible, so bringing her to this birthday party will kill two birds.

"That should be that," I say as I tuck away my phone. "And now we've got plans for the day after tomorrow."

"Seems like it."

"What about before that?" I ask. "What do you plan on doing?"

She sighs. "Working on VersaWear, nonstop."

I'm disappointed but completely understand. "What about at night?"

Her eyes widen. "Are you inviting yourself over?"

"That, or you can come visit me and Sir Ems."

She purses her lips. "Is this a date or a booty call?"

"A date."

"But it sounds like a booty call."

"What if I cook us dinner?" I suggest.

She grins. "Throw in a massage, and you've got yourself a date."

I promise her that massage, and we chat about nothing in particular until we land and then share a car that drops her off first.

Jumping out of the car, I open the door for Kendall and ask if I can help her get her suitcase to her apartment.

"Sure." She brushes her fingers over my hand as she hands me the suitcase.

"Wait for me," I tell the driver.

"How long?" he asks.

"A while," Kendall and I say in unison.

"I'll make it worth your while," I add.

The driver nods, and Kendall and I grin at each other the whole way to her door. Predictably, she invites me inside.

"Where do you want the suitcase?" I ask as I watch her take off her sneakers.

"Can you tuck it under the sofa?" She takes her socks off—exposing the bare feet of which I've been such a fan, especially after that foot job.

I deal with the suitcase, and when I come back, I could swear I see her hide a plastic bag inside a nearby hamper—a bag containing her socks.

Huh. Did I imagine that, or is she that much of a clean freak? If so, the island must've been more difficult for her than she let on.

"Would you like a tour?" she asks.

I nod, and she leads me into her living room, where a vintage tuba—or rather, sousaphone—is displayed as a centerpiece, surrounded by fashionable modern furniture.

"No TV?" I ask, looking around.

"Haven't had time for it."

"And no animals?" I ask, though the pristine pink velvet couch is a dead giveaway.

She shrugs. "Does my former boss count?"

"Sure. But he's not your problem anymore." I glance at her bare feet. "Where is your bedroom?"

She leads me into a room with a bed covered by chic monochrome bedding. It sits on top a cozy rug. Next to one of the pillows is a plushie in the shape of a penguin.

"That's Oswald," Kendall says, having followed my gaze.

"Is his last name Cobblepot?"

It must be the right thing to say because she kisses me, and we pull off each other's clothes with a desperation that shouldn't be there considering what happened so recently on the plane. Then again, the two of us are like baking soda and vinegar: put us together, and the fizzy chemistry becomes unstoppable.

"Lie down and spread your legs for me," I say hoarsely when we pull apart from the kiss. "I want to savor you."

She complies, her hazel eyes heavy-lidded.

I taste her with relish, and it's like coming home. Speaking of coming, I do not stop my ministrations until she comes three times for me, and then and only then do I enter her, moving slowly, thoughtfully, making eye contact the whole time.

Fuck me.

Something about this moment is different.

More sensual.

More mindful.

It's like with every thrust, we're becoming one. A whole that is better than the sum of its parts.

"I'm going to come," Kendall gasps, her pupils widening.

She bucks against me, and I instinctively speed up until I can't hold back anymore and I erupt into her, feeling her release all over me.

"You have to go, right?" she asks after we both recover enough to carry on a semi-coherent conversation.

"Sadly, yes. Randy has already done me a huge favor looking after Sir Ems beyond our original agreement. I promised I'd relieve him tonight."

She pouts prettily. "I seem to sleep better when you're around."

Has she forgotten how little we actually slept when we shared a bed? Then again, when I did sleep, it was pretty deep, especially considering how hot it was on the island.

"I could stay over tomorrow if you'd be okay with me bringing my dog."

She looks uncertain. "Will he make a mess?"

I shake my head. "He's a good boy. He hasn't made a mess since he was seven months old—which is the equivalent of a twelve-year-old kid. And before you ask, he didn't inherit such good behavior from me. I was a devil way beyond that age." Especially if you listen to my parents.

She chuckles. "You *were* a devil? Past tense?"

"That sounds like my cue to leave." I very reluctantly get up and get dressed—and when I catch her watching me, her expression is difficult to read.

Once I'm dressed, she puts on a robe and walks me to the door, which is where I kiss her goodbye before trudging to the car that's still waiting for me.

"Where to?" the driver asks.

I tell him, and we get going. A few minutes into the trip, my sister calls.

"Hey," she says, her voice sounding odd. "Sorry I couldn't take your call. I was on the stupid hike."

Stupid? She loves hiking. "Is everything okay?"

"No," she says.

I grip the phone tighter. "What happened?"

She blows out a breath. "I just got home from the

doctor. A tick attached itself to my shoulder, so I had to get it removed."

"Fuck."

"Yeah. I wore long sleeves and boots. The asshole managed to get me anyway."

"But the doctor removed it?"

"Yeah. They're going to test it for Lyme disease."

"Fucking fucker." I never would've thought I'd want to do violent things to a tick, but here we are. "Please take some time off. And don't worry about that dinner I texted you about. I'll—"

"Yeah, right," she says, sounding like her usual self. "Your new girlfriend will be there. A whole army of ticks couldn't keep me away."

"I mean it," I say firmly. "I'm ordering you to take it easy."

"And I will. But I'm not skipping that dinner. No way."

"Fine." When it comes to my little sister, I know which fights are worth it and which aren't. "Let me know as soon as the tests come through."

"Sure. Now if you don't mind, I'm going to go get some sleep."

"Of course. Talk to you tomorrow."

I hang up and start typing a query in my phone's search engine. My vet prescribed Sir Ems a pill that prevents tick bites. Should I have provided my sister with something similar?

Turns out, no. Such things only exist for dogs.

.   .   .

WHEN I STEP INTO MY APARTMENT, SIR EMS GREETS ME with such excited tail wagging you'd think it's been a decade since I left.

"I've missed you too," I tell him as I pet him and scratch behind his ears. "Next time, I'm taking you with me. You would've helped in case I really did end up having to hunt for survival."

Randy looks curious at this, so I tell him—but really Sir Ems—about what happened in detail, skipping only the intimate parts pertaining to Kendall.

"Glad you made it out safe," Randy says. "I'm going to go. Call me if you need my help again."

"Thanks." I pay the man, adding a huge tip on top of what I owe.

"Want to go for a walk before we head to bed?" I ask Sir Ems.

He gives me a look that speaks volumes, and in a British accent on top of that. "For a human—even of the Yank variety—you ask the daftest questions. As a dog, the day I refuse a walk is the day you can be sure that evil squirrels have succeeded in poisoning my brain."

CHAPTER 27

Kendall

WHEN I WAKE up and check my phone, there's a text from Ashton already waiting for me—an image of his dog, followed by:

We're very excited to see you tonight.

Shit. Should I back out? He's not my boyfriend—and can't be—but having him over with his dog confuses things.

Then again, he said he'd make me dinner. And that there would be a massage.

Feeling like a weak-willed ninny, I reply that I'm also excited… to see Sir Ems.

There.

I eat breakfast and log in to take care of my secret gig. I now need it more than ever to pay my bills. After a trip to the post office, I sit myself in front of the computer and work on VersaWear—until someone rings my doorbell.

What?

I check the time.

Wow. It's already six in the evening. I got so absorbed in my work that I missed lunch, and most of the day.

"Who is it?" I ask when I get to the door.

There's a cheerful, yippy woof outside the door.

I grin. "Sir Ems, is that you?"

"Indeed, gentle lady," Ashton says in a high-pitched voice with a British accent. "'Tis I, Sir Eats-Minced-Meat-a-Lot, at your service. Open posthaste, before my human and I succumb to the evil machinations of the squirrel menace."

I open the door, and my ovaries get smashed by Ashton's handsomeness—and the fact that he's holding a bouquet of roses.

Holy crap. I must've grown desensitized to his hotness after spending so much time together on the island, but after this short break, the full force of his beauty is hitting me like a freight train. That golden hair, that athletic physique, those gorgeously chiseled features...

"Here." He hands me the flowers and plants a kiss on my lips, one that makes my blood pressure spike and my panties dampen.

A small whine brings my attention to the dog, and I look down, cocking my head.

"Is he smiling?" I ask Ashton.

"It's a quirk of this breed," he answers. "And sure, I choose to think that he's smiling."

Sir Ems wags his tail as if to confirm his cheerful

mood.

"Well," I say. "Come in."

I was talking to Ashton, of course, but Sir Ems is the first to react: he trots regally inside, sniffing everything on his way.

"He won't cause mischief," Ashton says, noticing my worried expression.

A concerned bark rings out from the living room, contradicting Ashton's words.

Frowning, Ashton goes in—and starts cracking up.

I follow them and see why.

Sir Ems is barking at the sousaphone on display.

"Buddy, that's just a musical instrument," Ashton says soothingly.

Sir Ems pauses the barking but looks at the sousaphone distrustfully and then growls at it.

"Did you just get upset at your own refection?" Ashton asks.

Sir Ems looks at the shiny sousaphone again, then at his human, then back at the sousaphone, then back at Ashton.

Finally, the hackles on the back of the dog's neck relax, and the smile-like expression comes back, as does the tail wag.

Just then, someone rings the doorbell, and Sir Ems runs over to the door, barking up another storm.

I glance at Ashton. "No mischief?"

"Sorry," he says sheepishly.

"It's fine. I kind of like it." Though I considered myself as more of a dog person, that was all theory.

Now I know for a fact that I like dogs. Or at least corgis.

"We should go get that," Ashton says. "It's probably the groceries I ordered."

Ah. By the time I open the door, the delivery person has left—which instantly calms Sir Ems.

Ashton picks up the shopping bags and brings them to the kitchen.

"How do you feel about tacos?" he asks when I join him.

Upon hearing the word "tacos," Sir Ems almost jumps in joy.

"I was actually asking Kendall," Ashton tells the dog. "But you're going to get one, for sure."

"What kind of tacos?" I ask.

Given what might happen after, I'm not sure I want to eat something heavy, like pork.

"Roasted cauliflower, scallops, and shiitake mushrooms," Ashton says. "With my signature guacamole."

My stupid stomach rumbles.

Ashton grins.

"I skipped lunch," I explain defensively.

"Oh?" He takes out a pack of soft tortillas and crunchy taco shells. "Why?"

I explain how I got into a flow while working.

"That's great," he says. "Will you show me what you've got so far over dinner?"

"Sure." I get my laptop and then watch in hungry fascination as he fries the shiitake, sears the scallops, and assembles the tacos with the careful expertise of a chef in a Michelin-star restaurant.

When I taste the result, I moan in pleasure. "This is insane," I say after I swallow. "I don't think you're as good at training people as you are at this."

"That's not fair." He gives Sir Ems a taco. "You didn't give me a chance to train you."

"I guess." I taste the taco once again—and almost bite my tongue.

"Okay. Show me what you've been working on." He gestures at the laptop.

So I do, starting with the initial sketches I created earlier in the day and then going into the preliminary technical designs.

"What's next?" he asks.

"After I finish the tech packs, I'll need to source fabrics and materials."

"How long will the whole thing take?"

I shrug. "Depends what you mean by that. Getting to the sampling stage would usually take several weeks or longer, but I might be able to cut that down drastically if I live and breathe this project. But if you're talking about getting something into production and then stores, *that* will take much, much longer, so I won't even think about that."

He asks for more details, and like before, he has some good ideas, especially for someone who didn't go to a design school.

"I went to business school," he reminds me when I question him about that. "I didn't finish, but I learned enough. Not to mention, my own business is going well."

"Merely well. Understatement much?"

"I'm just saying that if you need help with the entrepreneurial aspects of this endeavor, I'd be happy to assist."

That assumes he'll be around when such skills will be necessary, but I dare not rely on that. Not when we're basically nemeses with benefits... who, I guess, aren't all that much at odds with each other anymore.

"Should I make dessert?" Ashton asks.

I shake my head. "Too full. I could really use a massage, though. My neck is stiff from working all day."

"Hold on." He cleans up the kitchen and sticks the plates into the dishwasher before turning back to me. "Should we go to the bedroom?"

My heart rate spikes. Trying to play it cool, I glance at the dog. "Is he coming with?"

"No. But if you have a spare pillow, or don't mind putting a couch cushion on the floor, he'd enjoy using that as a bed."

After a moment of thought, I designate a cushion for Sir Ems, then drag Ashton into the bedroom and kiss him the way I've wanted to from the moment he arrived.

His smile is smug as we separate. "So... is 'massage' a new euphemism for fucking?"

I roll my eyes. "You're going to do both: massage me and then fuck me."

He rubs his hands together. "Strip and lie down on your stomach."

I WAKE UP IN ASHTON'S ARMS, FEELING OBSCENELY content.

"Breakfast?" he murmurs, kissing my neck. "I can whip up the crepes that I was going to make last night for dessert."

It's tempting, but... "Thank you, but I'll just have cereal in front of my computer. Work is calling. And you need to go."

"That's dedication." He sits up. "What are we doing tonight?"

"The birthday party," I remind him. "I'll text you the details."

"Ah. Right." He stands up, and he's either oblivious to the fact that he's naked, or he's trying to make me horny on purpose. Again.

When we come out of the bedroom, Sir Ems is already waiting, tail wagging and smile contagious.

"Mind if I give him a leftover taco?" Ashton asks.

"You cooked it and brought the ingredients over," I remind him.

Nodding, Ashton swings by the fridge and gives the food to the dog—who proceeds to set a world record for wolfing down a taco.

"All right." Ashton leashes his best friend and walks over to the door. "See you later."

Before my lips can form the word "goodbye,"

Ashton claims them in a scorching kiss that makes me rethink the whole "I need to work" business. Sadly, I don't get a chance to voice anything out loud because by the time I've caught my breath, Ashton has already left.

Nothing left to do but pull myself together, grab that boring cereal, and start working.

MY PHONE RINGS.

I frown at it. Given the time, I've clearly lost myself in design again, to the tune of several hours. More importantly, the caller ID states "Mr. Boss."

"Hello?" I say, but what I really mean is: "This had better be important."

"Okay, you win," Tierre says in that voice he uses when he wants to sound compassionate, though it really comes across as condescending.

"Huh?"

"Yes, yes. I *can* be merciful," Tierre continues in that same tone. "If you want it back so bad, you can have it."

I glare at the phone. "Is this a butt dial?"

"Butt…" Tierre enunciates the word like he's savoring it. "What are you talking about?"

"Right back at you," I snap. "And hurry, I'm kind of busy."

He sucks in a breath. "How dare you? I call you to offer your job back, and you're being rude to me?"

"Ah. I get it now. How many assistants have quit on you so far?"

"My generous offer is withdrawn," he says but, tellingly, doesn't hang up. "You remain fired."

"Got it. I guess it works out because I'm out of the assistant business now, anyway."

With that, I hang up before I can say something I might later regret.

Realizing my heart is racing, I take a few calming breaths.

Did I just make a mistake?

No. I love designing, and I didn't like ninety percent of the menial tasks I had to do for Tierre.

In hindsight, I should've quit a year ago. Maybe even earlier.

A text from Ashton arrives in that moment, asking where and when we're meeting. I reply, set an alarm, gobble down leftover tacos, and dive back into work.

THE GLOBAL GRUB GROTTO IS A RESTAURANT THAT claims to specialize in delicacies from around the world, but in reality, it's known as the place where you can get the weirdest dishes in the city. The owner, Chef Lars, claims he tailors to the so-called adventurous eaters like my brother, but if you ask me, someone has simply watched *Fear Factor* one too many times.

As soon as I walk in, I smell something odd and unappetizing—with the most generous interpretation being that the restaurant has recently used a new and *very* strong cleaning product.

No. Must not think in that direction. It's Cameron's

birthday, and the last thing I want to do is yuck his yum.

"Are you here for the private event?" asks the hostess.

"Yes. Birthday." As if to prove it, I display my wrapped gift—a phone case I personally created for him from denim, canvas, and quilted cotton.

"And which of the menus are you going to be ordering from?" she asks. "Basic or adventurous?"

I sigh. "Basic, please."

She hands me the menu in question with a slight wrinkle of her nose. "Right this way."

She leads me past a display of desserts that are made to look like regular, everyday objects and into a big room with tables filled with people—some very familiar to me, like Mom and Dad, and some I've only seen at Cameron's other birthdays.

"Ken-doll!" my father shouts. "Come, we saved you a seat."

Shit. My brother is sitting with them also, which means I can't spare Ashton from a full-on "meet the parents" experience.

Forcing a smile to my lips, I kiss everyone and wish Cameron a happy birthday before handing him his gift.

"Thanks, sis." He unwraps the case, and everyone oohs and aahs as my brother ceremoniously takes out his phone and replaces his generic case with my creation.

"What do you think?" Dad asks him.

"Love it," Cameron says. Turning my way, he kisses my cheek. "Thanks again."

"So..." Mom looks around. "Where is your boyfriend?"

I grab a glass of water and take a big swig. "For the love of Manolo Blahniks, please, pretty please, don't call him that when he shows up. He's not my boyfriend and never will be. He's only here because Cameron wanted to talk shop with him today. That's all. He's even bringing a co-worker—who, before you ask, also isn't my boyfriend."

"The lady doth protest too much, methinks," Mom says.

Cameron looks at the entrance. "Is that him?"

I turn. Tall, blond, ridiculously handsome, and impeccably dressed—check, check, check, and check. "Yeah," I manage to say in a casual tone, as though my heart isn't suddenly dancing a jig in my chest.

"And who is that with him?" my brother asks, his voice sounding odd. "Is it his actual girlfriend?"

Great question because the beautiful blonde who walks in with Ashton is not acting like an employee at all. For starters, she punches Ashton's shoulder and rolls her eyes at something he says. Ashton then offers her his arm, and she places her slender hand through the crook of his elbow before they walk inside.

Finally—and most telling of all—there's something protective about the way he stares down any man who goggles at his... whoever she is.

And no, I don't want to rip her pretty hair out. At all.

"If that guy isn't your boyfriend, why do you look so jealous?" Mom asks pointedly.

"I do not. I'm just surprised, is all. When he said he was bringing his CTO, I imagined a dorky dude, not a fashion model."

And that surprise is definitely what's responsible for the bizarre tightness in my chest.

"Isn't that sexist?" Dad asks.

"Sure is," Mom replies. "But in Kendall's defense, women can get very catty when jealous."

How is that a defense? And... isn't that even more sexist than what I said?

"Hi," Ashton says as he and the model reach our table.

I leap to my feet and do my best to act like a normal human being. "Ashton, meet Mom, Dad, and my brother, Cameron."

"Hello, Kendall's dad." Ashton shakes Dad's hand. "And mom." He kisses her on the cheek—and she looks like her menopause has unpaused.

"Happy birthday, Cameron." He shakes my brother's hand and hands him a wrapped box.

"Thanks." My brother sets his gift on a nearby table and then nods at the model. "Will you introduce us to your... plus one?"

"Ah. Right," Ashton says. "This is my CTO, Jordan."

"Hi, all," Jordan says and bats her lashes at everyone

prettily. "I'm also this knucklehead's sister—in case you're wondering about the resemblance."

I'm so relieved I drop into my seat, and to my chagrin, my family members all sneak knowing looks at me.

"I can see the resemblance now that I know to look for it," I say, and it's true. And—maybe relatedly—I suddenly like Jordan, a lot, and not just because of the teasing way she handles Ashton.

It's something about the intelligence in her eyes. Or her smile. Which, come to think of it, is a lot like her brother's.

"I don't see any resemblance," Cameron says. "I think you both look unique."

Uh-oh. I take out my phone and write a quick text to my brother:

Don't even think about it. Henceforth, Jordan is officially covered by the pact.

Hearing his phone ding, Cameron sneaks a glance and looks very disappointed by my proclamation—which means it *was* necessary.

A waiter stops by and asks if we're ready to order.

"Give us a minute," Dad tells him.

Everyone studies their respective menus. Even on the so-called basic menu, the most palatable item I can find is haggis—a Scottish dish usually made from sheep's heart, liver, and lungs, which are mixed with oats and spices before getting cooked in the sheep's stomach. Apparently, the ban on importing this item was recently lifted, and thus it's on the menu here.

Ashton, who seems to be holding the adventurous menu, orders tacos with escamoles. I don't ask him to explain what that is.

Mom chooses a dish that features a century egg, and Dad gets an ominous-sounding black pudding. Both are on the basic menu, so I happen to know one is an egg that's been preserved to the point where the yolk has become green and the whites brown, and the other is—as the name hints at—blood mixed with oats.

"Is the kiviak imported or made locally?" Jordan asks and receives an approving look from my brother.

"Imported," the waiter says. "The chef has a relationship with the Inughuit."

"I'll have that," Jordan says.

"And I'll have the hákarl," my brother says.

The waiter leaves, and everyone discusses what their choice entails, though I kind of wish that they wouldn't. Kiviak turns out to be a bunch of small birds that have been fermented inside a seal carcass—because, of course—and hákarl is also a fermented treat, in this case shark meat that has been buried in gravelly sand and then hung to dry for several months. Oh, and the fun doesn't end there.

Escamoles is ant larvae.

"So, Ashton," Dad says when the excitement about our dishes subsides. "How did you and our daughter meet?"

"At the gym," he says. "I tried to train her, but she wasn't having it."

Every traitor from my family nods.

"Even when she was a baby, she didn't like to follow instructions," Mom says.

"Teaching her to ride a bike was the most trying time of my life," Dad says solemnly. "That and taking her to the dentist for the first time."

"At least you didn't try to teach her to play chess," my brother chimes in. "That was actual torture."

"Enough." I narrow my eyes at each of them. "We're changing the topic."

"What about you two?" Ashton asks my parents. "How did you meet?"

Oh, boy. I've never seen a worse case of "be careful what you wish for."

"You could say she was also a client of mine," Dad says with a grin.

Ashton arches an eyebrow while my brother and I exchange a "is this happening again?" look.

"My husband is a proctologist," Mom says gleefully.

Dad nods. "It's true. I had to study a long time to deal with assholes for a living."

Yep. Just like every other time this comes up.

"In fact," Mom continues, "it's safe to say we met after he saved my ass—literally."

Of course, she'd say that again. And he will say—

"And what an ass it was," Dad replies as expected. "A m-ass-terpiece."

I sigh. I know what's coming next, and how futile it would be to try and stop them.

"Have you guys ever heard proctologist jokes?" Mom asks.

A grinning Ashton shakes his head, as does his sister.

"Well then," my dad says. "I'll *rectify* that situation right now."

I groan, and Cameron rolls his eyes.

"Did you know that mine was the first profession to go digital?" Dad asks.

Ashton and his sister chuckle politely.

"Tell them what you'd say to a pirate, if you met one," Mom urges.

"Show me your booty," Dad says.

That one is new, but that doesn't make it good.

"Now tell them the difference between an accountant and a proctologist," Mom suggests.

Dad grins devilishly. "An accountant stares at spreadsheets while I stare at spread cheeks."

Cameron slowly shakes his head, and I don't get why he doesn't play the birthday card to put an end to this.

"You know what they call a sarcastic proctologist?" Mom asks.

"A smart-ass doctor," Dad replies.

Looking uncomfortable, Jordan and Ashton chuckle again. I bet they're wondering how many more of these there are—and the answer is: an infinite amount.

"How is a chiropractor different from a proctologist?" Mom asks.

"You go to the first to crack your finger," Dad says with a snort. "And the other if you need your crack fingered."

I blow out a breath.

Unperturbed, Mom tells them what Dad says when he walks into a bar: "Is this stool taken?" She then asks what his favorite medicine and food are, but to my huge relief, that is when our orders arrive and interrupt the answer, which happens to be ass-pirin and poo-nut butt-er, respectively.

When the waiters leave, I glance at Cameron's plate, which seems to be where the odd smell is coming from.

"Yeah, I know," my brother says. "The one problem with this dish is the ammonia smell." He puts a piece of fermented shark into his mouth and chews with clear relish. "The taste is worth it, I promise you."

"I'll take your word for it," I say and sample my own dish.

Interesting. It's rich, meaty, and nutty, with an earthy aftertaste. Reminiscent of liver pâté and meatloaf.

Ashton crunches into his taco and seems to enjoy it. Mom and Dad sing praises to their choices as well, and even Jordan seems to like her dish.

As much as it pains me to admit it—and despite the idea being completely out of the question—maybe she and Cameron would make a suitable match after all. In a parallel universe. Where she definitely isn't Ashton's sister.

"Back to jokes?" Mom suggests when the edge of everyone's hunger is blunted.

"Sorry, no," Cameron says. "I need to discuss some business with Ashton and Jordan."

"Boo," Mom says. "Work and birthdays don't mix."

"Yeah," Dad says. "You don't see me asking anyone to take off their pants."

Cameron frowns. "I thought everyone promised not to call me a workaholic today, of all days."

"Sorry," Mom and Dad say in unison.

"I want to go choose a dessert," Mom says. "They have a big display case of them."

"Great idea," Dad says. "I'll join you."

With that, they leave, which seems to be all the invitation Ashton needs to start talking about his app. Soon, he, Jordan, and Cameron seem to be speaking a foreign language, throwing out terms like "real-time suggesting," "natural-language processing," and "food-pairing algorithms."

"It sounds like you can really help us," Jordan finally says just as Mom and Dad return.

Cameron nods. "Sounds like it. Give me your email, and I'll have my assistant set up a meeting so we can discuss this in greater detail."

"Dessert picked," Mom announces as Jordan gives Cameron her card. "I'm going to order the one that looks like a little purse."

"And I'm getting the one that looks like a burger," Dad says. Looking at his half-eaten black pudding, he adds, "I'm actually craving a burger now."

"Did you like your dish?" Cameron asks Jordan.

"Yeah," she says. "But it makes me wonder—who first thought of fermenting these birds? And why?"

That's what she wonders? I'm curious as to who

thought of stuffing them into the skin of a seal, and what did that seal do to deserve it? Not hold a ball on his nose long enough?

"Forget birds," Ashton says. "How did someone come up with alcohol?"

Jordan grins. "Someone went, 'Here are some grapes. Let's have them spoil and drink *that*. Maybe something good will happen.'"

"Cheese is weird too," Cameron chimes in. "Here's some curdled milk. Tastes awful. Let's wait longer and see what happens."

"In general, I think whoever came up with the idea of drinking milk must've been a pervert," Dad says. "I mean, we take it for granted now, but someone had at some point looked at a cow and thought: 'I want to suck on *those* teats.'"

"Udders," Mom corrects him. "And don't forget that humans were lactose intolerant for a lot of our history, so perverts kept trying to drink milk until some lucky one had the mutation that let him digest it, and then he —because it must have been a man—passed the milk-drinking gene on."

"I think fermentation is still stranger," I say. "Have you ever seen how kombucha is made? My boss made me make it once, and there's a jellyfish-like thing involved."

"It's not a jellyfish. It's a Symbiotic Culture of Bacteria and Yeast, or SCOBY," Cameron says. "And it's edible."

"It didn't look edible," I say. At least no more so than a jellyfish, which is on the menu here, so there's that.

"Many things become edible if you're brave enough," Jordan says sagely.

"But you don't need to be particularly brave to eat SCOBY," Cameron replies. "I've eaten candy made from it. And jerky. All tasted fine."

I remind myself of today's yuck yum mantra and ponder out loud how the first SCOBY came to be.

Cameron shrugs. "Someone in ancient China left very sweet tea sitting out, some yeast and bacteria got into it and ate all the sugar, and then someone drank the result."

The waiter shows up and asks everyone if we want dessert.

Mom and Dad order while the rest of us tell him to come back in a couple of minutes, so we can go check out the display.

On the way to the dessert, Ashton leans in and whispers, "I love your parents."

"Yeah," Jordan says. "I do too."

"You do?" Cameron looks from brother to sister like they've just sprouted proctologists from their butts.

"Oh, yeah," Ashton says. "If you don't see it, you don't know how lucky you have it."

Jordan nods. "You can just tell they love each other very much. Super adorable."

"I guess you're right," I say.

My parents do love each other. Always have, despite

some people thinking that Mom just wanted Dad for his money. If she *were* a gold-digger, she would've left him after the malpractice suit that so drastically changed their financial situation, but she stuck with him and is actually helping him get back on his feet.

Note to self: avoid getting into that topic because Dad doesn't mind talking about it—probably so he can joke that when it comes to that lawsuit, assholes in both senses of the word were involved. More importantly, if Ashton learns that my parents are not helping me financially, he may wonder how I'll pay the bills now that I'm unemployed—which gets much too close to my secret project. Relatedly, I also need to make sure Ashton doesn't mention me losing my job to my family. I haven't told them because, again, they'll wonder how I'll pay my bills.

"I'm getting the Rubik's Cube-shaped one," Jordan says.

I scan the display. "I like the sponge cake." One made to look like a kitchen sponge, of course.

"I'm still pretty hungry," Ashton says. "I think I want the spaghetti with meatballs."

I grin. The version he's getting uses buttercream for spaghetti, chocolate truffles for meatballs, and strawberry cream as sauce. "Can I try it?" I ask.

"We should all try each other's desserts," Jordan suggests.

"In that case, I'll take the one that looks like a book," I say. "So I'll have something to share."

When we return to the table, the conversation turns

to food and stays that way until the end—because I do my best to keep it there and not on my employment situation.

Afterward, Ashton, Cameron, and Dad fight over the check until my brother plays the birthday card, which makes the others surrender.

"It was very nice meeting you," Ashton tells my parents, and I know he means it.

"Yeah," his sister says. "I've never had this much fun at a business meeting before."

"Thank you for coming," Cameron says. "I liked having a business meeting during my birthday party. I think I'll make it a new tradition."

My parents and I boo this last part, but our hearts aren't in it.

"Would you like to share a cab?" Ashton asks me.

The ears of my whole family perk up at this.

"Makes sense," I say. "We live two blocks away from each other." More like thirty-six, but who's counting?

"Right," Ashton says, eyes gleaming. "You're basically the girl next door."

My brother turns to Jordan. "Where do you live?"

"Uptown," she says vaguely.

"I'm taking my parents to Connecticut," he says. "I can drop you off on the way."

Damn it. Didn't he read my text?

"No, thank you," she says. "I'm meeting some friends for drinks."

If my brother is disappointed, he hides it well.

"Okay," Ashton says. "Let's go… neighbor."

He leads me out, and we jump into a cab.

"Your place or mine?" he asks. "Not that it matters, given that we practically live in the same building."

"Mine," I say. "And thanks for not putting me on the spot."

"No problem." He texts the dog sitter and then lays a hand on my thigh.

I tell the cab driver our destination, and as we get going, Ashton gives me a deep, hungry kiss—one that culminates in multiple orgasms when we finally get to my place.

CHAPTER 28

Ashton

I WAKE up with Kendall wrapped around me.

Her alarm clock is blaring. She grabs the thing and tosses it at the wall, which stops the noise.

Smiling, I kiss her shoulder. "Didn't you want to start working nice and early?"

"Shut up," she grumbles. "Or I'll throw *you*."

I shrug and close my eyes, only to open them again a couple of hours later.

Kendall sits up. "Why did you let me oversleep?"

I extend an arm toward the poor, broken alarm clock. "That was you."

"Ah. Right." She gets out of bed. "I'd better get to work ASAP."

Truth be told, I have a meeting with Jordan in a half hour, which barely gives me enough time to get myself together. That is why I let Kendall usher me out—but not before we make plans for me to come back that very evening.

. . .

My day is very busy. After talking with my sister, I do a friend a huge favor and take on a new client—the guy who was recently appointed Director of the FBI. After that, I head over to Essence, where my team records me as I do my back workout—something that will become an instructional video for the app.

When I return to Kendall's place, I bring Sir Ems with me and make dinner, just like the night before the birthday outing. Not surprisingly, Kendall and I have the most mind-blowing sex yet.

For the next two weeks, a pattern emerges. I train celebrities, exercise like a fiend, and field inevitable fire drills that—alongside the unwanted wealth that so pleases my parents—are the downside of overseeing a successful fitness app. Kendall works on her design project, even on weekends, but has me come over daily to feed her and then feast on her. The only difference from day to day is that the sex is impossibly improving, and relatedly, I'm growing more convinced that whatever is happening between us is very serious.

In fact, when I talk to my sister the following Monday, without any preamble, I ask, "When is it too soon to ask someone to move in with you?"

"If it hasn't been a year, it's too soon," she says. "By my calculations, you've only been officially dating for two weeks."

"A year?" Marcus contrived to get Emma to move in with him two milliseconds after they met.

"Even after a suitable length of time," my sister continues, "it helps if you've already met each other's family and friends."

"That's half-done." I pour myself a glass of water. "You were there."

"Right. And if you two come to visit Mom and Dad with me next week, the parent angle will be completely covered."

Ah. "Nice try. No." Having Kendall meet our parents is a lose-lose proposition. She won't like them—that's a given—but if they like her, it might actually make me like her less. But if they don't like her, it will make me upset with them—or more upset than I already am.

"Fine," Jordan says. "I guess their being in Boston makes her not meeting them somewhat forgiven."

"Especially if she doesn't know a trip there is a possibility," I say. "So don't tell her... or her brother."

Jordan and Cameron have been working together, so it's a real possibility.

"I obviously won't," she says. "How could you even hint otherwise?"

"Sorry. Anyway... do you think us moving in together is a good idea?"

"Depends," she says. "Do you love her?"

I nearly choke on my water. "No."

Or rather, I don't know. I do have feelings for her, tender ones, but I'm not ready to examine them closely because I get the feeling that Kendall is not "all in" when it comes to our relationship. If I had to guess, I'd say she still doesn't believe me about my three-year abstinence. Now, if she says yes to moving in with me, then maybe—

"That wasn't a very convincing 'no,'" Jordan says.

I sigh. "Next question."

"Do you openly talk finances?" she asks. "That's another important prerequisite."

Is it? I frown. "We don't really talk about money. She seems to avoid the topic, in fact. For what it's worth, moving in with me would make financial sense for her since she's trying to get her business off the ground."

Her parents help her out, I know, but I can tell she's the type of person who doesn't want to abuse such help.

"I'd wait at least a few more months," Jordan suggests.

I blow out a disappointed breath. "You're probably right."

"I always am."

With that, she hangs up.

Sir Ems trots over and gives me a soulful stare that seems to say, "My dear chap, if you do decide to move in with the pretty-smelling human, make sure she throws away the cat-like abomination that is her old sousaphone."

A WEEK LATER, KENDALL ASKS ME TO COME OVER A HALF hour early, and when I do, she's wearing an orange jumpsuit that puts all her curves on display—and makes my dick instantly hard.

"Is this the prototype?" I ask.

She only recently received the fabrics to play around with, so I didn't expect her to have something wearable so soon.

"This is more of a mock-up," she says. "I'll have the actual prototype done in a couple of weeks."

"Still," I say with a smile. "We should celebrate."

"Sure." She grins. "But help me get out of this thing."

As I do, I marvel how she got into it in the first place. Most of the mock-up is held together by enough pins to make a girlfriend for a porcupine.

Once she is out and therefore almost naked, I can't help but carry her to the bedroom, barbarian style, where we start the celebrations with a couple of orgasms.

Afterward, we head over to the nearest high-end sushi place because Kendall has a craving. Predictably, the place is packed, so I bring out my wallet and sneak the hostess a couple of hundreds.

"I'll give you the next table," she says.

"Thanks."

I lead Kendall outside to wait and ask, "Did you ever have a roommate?"

It's a roundabout way to test the "move in" waters, but I've got to start somewhere.

"Sure, for a minute in college," she says. "I hated it."

Fucking hell. How do I pivot this so that—

"Kendall?" says an attractive older woman passing by.

Kendall turns, and her eyes widen. "Catherine. Hi. How are things going?"

Catherine smiles. "If that's an awkward way to ask if Tierre regrets firing you, the answer is a resounding yes."

Ah. So this is someone from Kendall's old job. Given the fashionable way the lady is dressed, it tracks.

"I suspected so," Kendall says. "But of course, we both know he'd never admit that."

"Oh, yeah. But hey, in his defense, when the rumors began about you putting together your own line, he claimed he let you go so you could 'spread your wings.'"

"Rumors?" Kendall asks.

Catherine shrugs. "A bunch of celebs that he knows told him they're awaiting your VersaWear with bated breath."

Kendall narrows her eyes at me. "Have you been plugging VersaWear more?"

I nod. "And I'm not sorry. When I believe in something, it's hard for me not to tell people."

Catherine turns my way, clearly just registering my presence. "Are you Kendall's agent?"

Kendall frowns. "You know perfectly well who he is."

"I do?" Catherine arches a bushy eyebrow. "And who is he?"

"Is this a joke?" Kendall looks at me. "You know her." She turns to Catherine. "You know him."

"I'm sorry, fashionista," I say. "I've never met Catherine before."

"It's true." Catherine gives me a thorough once-over. "He's the kind of man I'd remember."

"This isn't funny." A muscle in Kendall's jaw ticks. "You told me to see him."

"I did?" Despite copious Botox standing in the way, Catherine's forehead crinkles.

"Yes. Three years ago. You said to see him to rid myself of mopiness, remember?"

Catherine shakes her head. "I've no idea what you're talking about."

"He was working at Essence," Kendall says insistently.

Catherine shrugs, looking confused.

"You called him Ash at the time?"

Wait a second. I completely forgot that she came to see Asher the day we first met. So this was the woman who referred her?

Catherine waves a manicured hand toward me. "This man isn't Ash. I just saw the real Ash the other day, and he couldn't look like this even if he got all the plastic surgery in the world."

Kendall turns my way, her eyes wide. "So... you've never fucked this woman?"

My mouth goes slack. "What the hell?" We were just talking personal trainers, so how did this escalate so quickly? Unless... "Catherine, do you sleep with your trainer? Ash?"

"Who doesn't?" Catherine says with a shrug.

I turn to Kendall. "I'm not that Ash. Actually, I never even go by Ash."

Kendall staggers back, eyes even wider. "I guess... I've never heard anyone call you Ash."

"Because they don't." I face Catherine. "Am I correct in thinking the Ash in question is Asher Diggle?"

Catherine takes a step back. "Yes, but I don't want to get him into trouble."

I turn to Kendall. "So... when you said you had a friend who told you that I sleep around, was it Catherine?"

Catherine snorts. "Ash doesn't just sleep around. He fucks *everyone*. How else do you think a trainer that inept could have such a big roster of repeat clients?"

Something on my face must scare Catherine because she mutters a couple of excuses and rushes away.

I turn my fury to Kendall. "You actually believed such a thing about me? That I slept with every training client?"

Kendall's face is pale, but she stubbornly says, "That's what it sounded like."

"And you believed it until this moment? Even after getting to know me?"

She jams her hands under her armpits. "When I brought it up, you didn't deny it."

"I thought you were talking about sleeping around in college!" I realize my voice is raised, but I can't help it.

"College?" she asks in disbelief. "That's what you meant?"

"Yes. I told you. I'm not as much of a manwhore as you think." I drag in a breath. "Is this why you had such a hard time believing that I wasn't with anyone for three years?"

She looks stunned. "Is that *really* the case? You haven't been with anyone else since that night?"

"Yes." What will it take for this woman to fucking trust me?

Suddenly, something else hits me. This Ash misunderstanding is why she ghosted me three years ago—as in, for no reason at all. What's worse is, even now, even with everything clarified, she doesn't seem to trust me.

"I didn't see Ash to get laid, by the way," she says. "In case that's what you're thinking."

I didn't until now, but—

My phone rings and I want to ignore it, but the ringtone is "The Imperial March," which means it's my father calling.

And he never calls me. My mother, sure, but never this late.

"I have to take this," I tell Kendall tersely and pick up. "Hey. Is something wrong?"

"Yes," my father says grimly. "It's your sister. She was just rushed to the hospital."

CHAPTER 29
Kendall

AS ASHTON PICKS up the phone, I can see that he's angry about the Ash misunderstanding, and he has a right to be. As I process this new information, I feel progressively shittier. I can't even fathom how pissed I'd be if our roles were reversed.

Whatever Ashton hears on the other end of the phone call makes all the blood leave his face.

"What happened?" he demands.

I strain to hear, but I can't.

"Allergic to what?" Ashton shouts.

I can't hear the answer to this either, but Ashton grits out, "She's your fucking daughter. It's your job to know."

Okay, so I guess it's one of his parents, and the person in trouble is his sister.

My already-hammering heart speeds up. I really like Jordan, and if something bad has happened to her—

"Did they let Mom ride in the back?" Ashton half asks, half demands.

"Good," he says next. "Keep me posted. I'm heading to the airport now."

Hanging up, he looks at me, eyes wild. "Jordan had an allergic reaction. Dad doesn't know to what. She's being driven to the hospital as we speak. I'm going over there."

"Which hospital?" I ask.

"Boston Medical Center," Ashton replies as he steps over to the curb and hails a cab.

I blink. "Boston?"

"She went to visit our parents," he says over his shoulder.

Oh.

A cab stops and he jumps in. On impulse, I join him.

"What are you doing?" he demands.

"Coming with you," I say with a confidence I don't feel.

"Did you not hear? It's in Boston."

"Right," I say. "I don't mind the trip."

"It's going to be dangerous." Before I can clarify as to how, he tells the cabbie to get us to JFK and promises him a hundred-dollar tip if he can make it there in a half hour.

"Make it three hundred," the cabbie counters. "And if I get a ticket, you pay it."

"Deal." Turning to me, he says, "Now please get out."

"No." I cross my arms over my chest. "Speeding doesn't scare me. In fact, it sounds kind of fun."

"You're slowing me down," he says. "Please just—"

"Can you just take me? Please?"

"Fine. I don't have time to talk you out of it." Turning to the cabbie, he says, "Let's go."

The guy punches the gas, and we torpedo forward.

I bite my lip and sneak a glance at Ashton. "Can we talk?"

"No," he says without looking up from his phone. "You've slowed me down enough already. I've got to make arrangements with my dog sitter and get plane tickets."

Ah. "Okay. Get me one too? I'll pay you back."

He grumbles something unintelligible, still without looking up, and stays on his phone for the next fifteen minutes—which makes him miss the car-chase-like maneuvers the cabbie pulls on FDR Drive.

"Did you get them?" I ask him when he finally looks up.

He nods. "If we make it there in a half hour, we'll have twenty minutes to board."

In other words, our chances are pretty slim.

"I have TSA PreCheck," I say, trying to stay positive. "Do you?"

"Yes," he says, then winces as the cab zooms across traffic from the middle to the right lane, cutting off a giant truck in the process.

I want to remind the cabbie that if we're dead, he won't get paid, but I don't, as that might piss off Ashton even more.

Then again, maybe I should say something. The

cabbie cuts off a bus and nearly collides with a Tesla Y, all in the matter of a millisecond.

Meanwhile, Ashton looks so worried I can't help but put a hand on his shoulder.

Frowning, he shrugs off my hand. The rejection stings, but I dare not ask if he's acting this way because of the Ash debacle, or if he's too stressed for touching right now in general.

"She's going to be okay," I say as soothingly as I can.

Ashton gives me a sideways look. His voice is tense. "We don't know that."

"Don't EMTs have EpiPens? That's what she needs."

He clenches his teeth. "She asked me to go with her. Maybe if I had, her life wouldn't be in danger right now."

"That makes no sense."

In reply, he checks his phone and frowns. I sneak a peek at his screen and see him texting his dad.

You there yet?

No reply comes for a few silent minutes, so Ashton makes a call, but no one picks up.

"Call the hospital," I suggest. "They should be able to say if she was admitted."

"Thanks." He looks up the number and calls it. After a terse conversation, he hangs up with a curse.

"They said it could take up to an hour to triage her, then half an hour to register and admit. And who knows how soon after that she'll actually see a doctor."

"We might get there before that," I say.

He frantically taps at his phone, then nods. "The

flight is an hour and ten minutes. The cab ride from BOS to BMC is fifteen minutes without traffic."

"Call your dad again."

Ashton does, then tries his mom—to no avail.

By the time he finally gets through, we have reached our destination, so Ashton tosses a bunch of money at the cab driver and stays on the phone as we rush through security.

"Did you hear that?" I ask him when an announcer mumbles something along the lines of, "Last call for Boston flight."

Nodding, Ashton grabs my hand and launches into a sprint.

Panting, I do my best to keep up, and we just barely make it before the gate closes.

"So? What did you learn?" I ask once we're in our seats and I've caught my breath. I'm still sweaty from the mad dash, though, and more than a little annoyed that Ashton looks as cool as if he's been lounging on the couch instead of sprinting at full speed through half the airport.

I guess being in crazy good shape pays off in all kinds of situations.

"She did get epinephrin," Ashton says. "But she's still pretty swollen. They're waiting for her to get admitted."

"Ah." I buckle myself in.

Ashton hides his phone and sits in tense silence as the plane takes off.

Why is he not talking? Is it worry about his sister, or is he still mad at me?

I wrack my brain for something to ease the tension, but the best I can come up with is a suggestion to order some food.

"Right," he says. "We never ate that sushi."

I order the overpriced turkey and Swiss sandwich, while he gets the chicken Caesar wrap.

We eat in silence. My sandwich tastes like paint chips, and I'm not sure if that's because of the lower air pressure, the airline's crap sandwich-making skills, or the fact that Ashton is still visibly upset—for which I can probably take most of the blame.

"Hey," I say when the meal is over. "Can we talk about that whole Ash misunderstanding?"

His frown deepens. "Not now. Please."

"Right. Makes sense." And it sucks ass, but I can't exactly *make* him talk. And maybe he's right not to want to hash out things now. He might be too worried about Jordan to talk calmly and rationally.

Still, in my head, I play out the possible conversations that we might have, and they only end up making me feel worse about the whole thing.

As soon as we land, it's full speed ahead again. Talking on his phone with one hand and grasping my hand in the other, he pulls me through the crowds of passengers. His touch, though hurried and careless, grounds me. He only releases me once we're settled into another cab.

"What did they say?" I ask after Ashton offers the

current cab driver the same deal he made with the one in NYC.

"She just got admitted," he says. "Waiting for a doctor."

"I see."

The rest of the ride happens in more silence, but at least it's blissfully quick.

When we get to the emergency room, three people jump from their seats and approach us: two older adults who are likely Ashton's parents and an attractive woman about my age. All three of them are dressed in that understated yet posh way that all but screams "old money."

When Ashton spots the younger woman, he halts in his tracks, and his expression darkens—an impressive feat, given his mood on the way here.

"Gwyneth," he says in a voice so icy it makes the way he's been talking to me during this trip seem warm and fuzzy. "What the fuck are you doing here?"

The older woman who's most likely his mother clutches her pearls, literally. "Is such vulgar language necessary?"

Ashton's reply sounds like a low growl, and Gwyneth takes a step back before saying in a breathy voice, "I happen to know Jordan. We took Intro to Computer Science together. And Intro to C++."

"Yeah, sure." Ashton's voice drips with sarcasm. "You're practically BFFs—except for the part where she hates your fucking guts."

"You're upsetting your mother," his—I presume—

father says coldly. "If you must know, I invited Gwyneth after you told me you were coming here. I didn't realize you'd have company." He gives me a cool once-over. "I had hoped that maybe you'd come to your senses and—"

"Do not finish that sentence," Ashton snaps, then turns to the young woman. "Gwyneth, you'd better go."

"No," his mother says. "She's been useful. I want her to stay."

"And how has she been useful?" Ashton demands.

"She got us access to the hospital system," his mother says. "Told us which doctor Jordan's speaking with and what university he got his degree from."

Ashton whirls on Gwyneth. "You hacked into the hospital's system? You realize that can get you a visit from the FBI?"

His father finally looks at me. "Aren't you going to introduce us to your friend?"

Ashton's jaw flexes. "Later. Right now, I'm going to see my sister."

Grabbing my hand again, he strides over to the reception desk, where we learn where to find Jordan and provide our IDs to get visitors' passes.

A short walk later, we stop next to a bed with a swollen-looking Jordan—who beams a megawatt smile at her brother and then at me.

"You're here," she says, her words slightly slurred.

He puts his hand over hers. "Of course."

"You really didn't have to come all this way," she says. "This is just allergies."

He gives her a glare. "You know anaphylaxis can kill you, right?"

She sighs. "So the doctor just said."

"What else did he say?" Ashton demands.

"He thinks I reacted to my morning bacon."

"Bacon?" he asks incredulously.

She nods. "Said this might happen if I eat any meat from a mammal. But obviously, more tests are needed to be sure."

"All... mammals?" Ashton looks dubious.

"I know," she says. "If I were a cannibal, I'd be screwed."

Ashton frowns. "This is serious."

"I know," Jordan says. "The next time I get tuna, I'll have to make sure it's dolphin free for the sake of self-preservation."

"How could you just become allergic to meat all of a sudden?" he asks. "You've always eaten it without any problems."

"It's that stupid tick," Jordan says. "That's what clued the doctor in. He thinks I developed something called alpha-gal syndrome—and no, that doesn't mean I'm the type of gal who can lead a pack of werewolves."

Ashton runs a hand through his hair. "I've never heard of that."

"Me neither," Jordan says.

"I'm so sorry," I chime in. "That sounds horrible."

Jordan waves that away. "I can still eat fowl and seafood. Or maybe I'll become vegan—and finally prove that I'm better than everyone else."

"Whatever diet you decide on, I know a good nutritionist who can help you make a meal plan," Ashton says.

Jordan wrinkles her nose. "Speaking of unpleasant things, did you run into our parental units and Gwyneth on your way here?"

"Yes." He grimaces. "I can't believe Dad called her."

"I can," Jordan says. Turning my way, she adds, "Not sure if Ashton filled you in, but Gwyneth is the woman our parents wanted him to marry. They started pushing for it almost as soon as Ashton started dating her back in college, and they kept pushing for it even after Ashton broke up with her. They just couldn't accept that Ashton wasn't ready for such a serious commitment, and especially not with a stage-five clinger like Gwyneth."

Seeing my shocked expression, she nods. "I'm not kidding. And telling us whom to marry is just the tip of the iceberg. They wanted us to go to the school they chose, get jobs they approved of, and—"

"And your life would only be the better for it," says their father, who's clearly part ninja.

I turn and see both of his parents here, but thankfully, Gwyneth is not with them.

Which is good, because, for no reason that I can explain, I want to locate a scalpel and stab a bitch.

CHAPTER 30

Ashton

"SO WHAT DID THE DOCTOR SAY?" Mom demands.

Jordan tells them the same thing she told us, and our parents vow to get second, third, and fourth opinions.

"So," Dad says to me when we've covered everything about Jordan's condition. "You still owe us an introduction."

He and Mom look at Kendall pointedly.

Fuck. Why did I let her come with me?

"Relax," Jordan says. "I met Kendall's parents. Her dad is a doctor, and her mother does charity work."

"Oh," our parents say in unison and look at Kendall a lot more approvingly, which, of course, pisses me off.

"It's nice to meet you," Kendall says politely and shakes both of their hands.

What follows next feels a lot like an interrogation,

by the end of which I get the feeling that my parents are ready to replace Gwyneth with Kendall.

I, on the other hand, feel unsure about her for the first time since she ghosted me—but not because of said approval, as I would've expected. As it turns out, I couldn't care less what my parents think of her, one way or another. However, now that I know my sister is okay, I can finally process the whole Ash debacle, and the more I think about it, the more I hate it that Kendall didn't trust me—and kept thinking the worst of me even after we got to know each other.

Kendall's phone rings.

"Will you please excuse me?" she says. "It's Emma. She and Marcus just came back from their honeymoon."

"Of course," Jordan says. "Go."

When Kendall leaves, Mom gives me a dirty look. "Marcus—as in, your friend, Marcus Carelli?"

The fact that I didn't help my parents snag a billionaire son-in-law via Jordan is one of the many grievances I have to deal with.

"Can I get you anything?" I ask Jordan. "Maybe a drink or a snack?"

"Yeah. Can you get me a Jell-O cup? Green flavor."

I purse my lips. "Are you allowed gelatin if you have this alpha-gal thing? It might come from mammals."

She pouts. "This is going to take some getting used to. Bring me an animal cracker. It might be the closest I'll get to eating animals from now on."

"I'll go get some." After I make sure they're vegan, that is.

I walk briskly and spot Kendall still speaking on the phone nearby.

Should I call Marcus?

No. Maybe later. Right now, I need to get animal crackers and figure out where Kendall and I stand.

Turns out, the brand of animal crackers they sell here is vegan, so I pay for them and head back—which is when Gwyneth steps into my path.

"Can we talk?" she asks, smoothing a hand over her sleek brown hair.

I blow out a breath. "What about?"

"Us," she says.

Fucking hell. "There is no us. And there won't be. You know that."

Her eyes gleam. "Because of Kendall?"

I frown. "How do you know her name?"

"I know a lot more than that."

Translation from crazy speak: she probably hacked the hospital again, learned the name from Jordan's visiting record, and then stalked Kendall online.

"My sister is waiting for me," I say. "Have a nice life."

"Wait," Gwyneth says. "Don't go."

I wave the crackers. "Jordan is waiting for this." And more importantly, we have nothing to talk about.

"Your parents will never approve of her," Gwyneth says.

I shrug. "Not that it's any of your business, but in

fact, they like her just fine. Not that I care." The opposite, in fact.

"They won't like her once they learn what she does," Gwyneth says.

"Why not? Mom loves fashion, and Dad only cares about—"

"Not that," she snaps. "Her other business. The one for perverts."

"What the fuck are you talking about?"

Gwyneth smiles triumphantly. "You don't know, do you?"

I narrow my eyes. "Know what?"

She takes out her phone and types something in before showing me the screen. "Do these look familiar?"

I look at the URL first. It's the website porn stars use to milk money from their fans. This specific page belongs to someone named Candy Berlin, and all she's posted there are feet.

Tons and tons of pictures of feet.

Wait a second.

Those are familiar-looking feet, and not just because of the taupe-colored nail polish, and the two silvery toe rings, and the golden anklet.

I know these feet.

I like them.

I came on them.

These are Kendall's, but—

"She sells her dirty socks as well." Gwyneth wrinkles her nose. "Or if you have serious cash to burn, she can sell you her used Manolo Blahniks."

Sells used socks? I *have* noticed her putting worn socks into plastic bags a couple of times. I thought it was some neat freak tendency, or some weird girl thing where she was afraid that I might smell something I shouldn't, but she's selling them?

"If you don't believe me, I can show you how I found this," Gwyneth says. "It was pretty trivial, actually. All I had to do was—"

"Now, Gwyneth, listen to me very carefully." I let my turbulent emotions show in my tone. "If you mention this to anyone again—or so much as google Kendall's name—I will be talking to my new client, who happens to be Director of the FBI."

She pales. "You wouldn't want your client to know that your girlfriend is a—"

"If you finish that sentence, I'll call him right now." Just to show her I'm not bluffing, I pull up his contact in my phone and turn the screen toward her.

"Look, I just thought it was something you should know," Gwyneth says.

"And now I do. But if anyone else finds out—even if not through you—I'm making that call, and you'd better pray you didn't leave a digital footprint when hacking this hospital."

She turns even paler. "I can't believe I actually thought you and I could be together again."

"I can't believe you thought so either. I told you we were done, and I meant it." I don't add that after this conversation, even if an apocalypse wiped out all other women on the planet, I would sooner let humanity die out than be with her.

With a huff, Gwyneth turns on her heel and rushes out of the cafeteria.

I take a seat on the nearby chair, take out my phone, and pay the exorbitant fee required to see Candy Berlin's feet once again.

Yep.

Still there.

A part of me thought that maybe Gwyneth had somehow faked the page—though I now realize that was a last-ditch hope at best. I mean, where would Gwyneth have found so many pictures of Kendall's feet?

So it must be true. Here is yet another thing Kendall didn't trust me with, though I guess in this case, it's more understandable. She was probably worried that I'd be jealous, and she was right.

Just thinking about some assholes looking at—or sniffing—Kendall's feet makes me want to smash their noses into their faces. And yes, I know this reaction is over the top. I mean, if she went to a beach or wore sandals, everyone would see her feet... right? Then again, maybe not. If I were there, they wouldn't dare look at them. Certainly, no one should be sniffing anything—though if someone were to do any sniffing, that someone had better be me.

I leap to my feet.

Kendall and I need to have some words.

Walking fast, I return to my sister, but Kendall isn't there. Nor are our parents.

"Kendall didn't come back after that phone call," Jordan says without my asking.

"I see." I give her the crackers. "How are you feeling?"

"Much better. In fact, they promised to discharge me in a few minutes, so I told Mom and Dad they could head home."

And they went? Figures. Though in their defense, Jordan looks a lot less swollen, and they know I'm still here.

"Did something happen?" Jordan asks. "You look upset."

"Long story," I say tightly. "I need to speak with Kendall."

"Go find her then," Jordan says. "Then come back and give me a full report."

"You're going to be okay alone?" I ask, my tone softening.

She waves her phone at me. "I've got something I need to take care of, anyway."

"I'll be right back." I step away and look around, but I don't see Kendall anywhere.

I head in the direction she went earlier, and then I spot her—and blink a few times because, weirdly, she's talking to her brother.

What is he doing here?

Doesn't he live in New York?

As I get closer, I hear Kendall ask him that exact question in a tense tone.

"Jordan and I work together," he replies. "When I heard she was in trouble, I got here as soon as I could."

What the fuck? Is he dating my sister?

"I thought we agreed: she's off limits," Kendall says angrily.

My thoughts exactly.

"And why is that?" Cameron demands. "Because her brother is your boyfriend?"

"No. I told you, he's not my boyfriend. We're just—"

She stops speaking, probably because she's noticed Cameron's eyes widening at my approach. She turns. "Ashton. I—"

"No," I say evenly. "Please finish that sentence. We're just what? Nothing of consequence? Merely fuck buddies? What were you going to say?"

Looking uncomfortable, Cameron says, "I'm going to check on your sister."

I glare at him. If the fucker hurts her in any way, he's dead meat.

Before I can voice that sentiment, Cameron hurries away, leaving me and Kendall in a staring contest.

"I know about Candy Berlin," I say when I'm sure her brother is out of earshot.

She gapes at me. "How?"

"Is that all you care about?" I demand.

"No. I… just didn't expect you to say *that*."

"And I didn't expect to hear you tell your brother that I mean nothing to you. After we've been together all these weeks—and after you learned that I wasn't Ash. Which you should've realized long ago."

"The Ash thing was clarified only a couple of hours ago," she says defensively. "I didn't even get the chance to—"

"I heard about the Candy Berlin thing two minutes ago, and that is how long it took me to know I still want to be with you. Except I apparently wasn't with you. It was all my imagination."

"Ashton... I—"

"Don't," I say coldly. "I'd like you to go. Please. I'll call you a limo and make sure a ticket home is waiting for you at the airport."

Turning on my heel, I leave.

CHAPTER 31

Kendall

I CRY all the way home, trying to process everything that's happened and failing miserably.

Once I'm safely ensconced in my apartment, I call Emma, but she doesn't pick up, probably because it's late.

I cry myself to sleep.

In the morning, a phone call wakes me up. At first, I think it's Ashton and my heart leaps with hope, but it's Emma.

"Hey," I say, rubbing the sleep from my eyes.

"Hey," Emma says. "I heard about you and Ashton."

"You did?" I squeeze the phone tighter.

"Yesterday, on his way home, he called Marcus."

The edges of my phone dig into my hand. "And what did he say?"

"I'm not supposed to say anything." Emma sounds miserable. "Marcus wasn't even supposed to tell me."

"Oh." A lump invades my throat. "I understand."

"Are you crying?" Emma says on a gasp.

"No." I wipe away the errant moisture under my eyes. When did it get there? "Why would I?"

"Listen... How about you tell me what happened from your point of view? Maybe I don't need to tell you any secrets."

So I do that, including, finally, fessing up to her about my secret business.

"I almost understand them looking at your feet," Emma says. "But buying dirty socks? Used footwear?"

"That's what you ask me after all that?"

"Sorry," she says. "It does kind of explain why you get yourself so many pricey shoes. It's a business expense."

"Sure. We'll call it that." It has nothing to do with me having an almost orgasmic experience when shopping in a high-end shoe store. Nothing at all.

"How did you get into... that?" she asks.

"Remember my roommate from college?"

"The one you hated?"

"Yeah. She was doing the same thing, so when I needed the money, I decided why the hell not?"

"Why did you need the money?" she asks. "I thought your parents were helping you."

I sigh. "My parents got into financial trouble shortly after we graduated—a malpractice suit in combination with lapsed malpractice insurance pretty much wiped them out—and I didn't want to accept handouts from Cameron."

"Oh. Why didn't you tell me?"

"You had your own money problems. And I wasn't sure how you'd feel about me selling my body."

"Even if you were truly selling your body—which your little side business doesn't qualify as—I'd still think of you as my friend," she says solemnly.

"There's also the part where you know my parents," I say, wiping another—this time, relieved—tear. "They'd be ashamed if they knew you'd found out about their financial issues. Dad loves talking about the lawsuit, but how it bankrupted them—not so much."

"Oh, gotcha. Of course. Next time I see them, I'll pretend I don't know."

"Thanks," I say. "Now it's your turn to tell me things."

"Well, you're right. Ashton *is* upset," she says. "The mere fact that he called Marcus is a testament to that. Apparently, they don't *usually* talk about feelings. They use each other as punching bags instead."

Fuck. "So… you think that means it's over?"

"Is that what you want?" she says softly.

"What difference does it make? I fucked it up. Whatever 'it' was."

"Well, upset or not, he did want to move in with you —and that's a serious step. From my experience, marriage follows that, so I doubt he'd give up on you after your first fight."

"Wait. He wanted to *move in* with me?" I shout.

"Oops. That was one of the things I wasn't supposed to tell you."

"But… move in?"

"Didn't you tell me he's been spending the night with you every night?"

"Well, yeah. He and his dog."

"And he works during the day, right?"

"Sure."

"So... how would your life be all that different if you did move in together?"

My head spins. "That's not the point. We weren't even dating."

"That's not how he saw it. He told Marcus you were his girlfriend... until yesterday."

This is ridiculous. "Why does the 'until yesterday' part make me so upset? I didn't even know I was his girlfriend."

"Maybe because you want to be?"

Do I? All my conversations with Ashton play in front of my mind's eye. And the smiles. And the laughs. And the dinners, the massages, the toe-curling orgasms...

"Of course, I do," I admit with a sigh. "But I was an idiot. I'm not sure if I can fix it now."

"It's worth a shot," Emma says. "And I've got an idea of how you can go about it."

I listen with bated breath, and as she tells me, I know that I'll try her idea, which will either end with me getting Ashton back or my first-ever concussion.

CHAPTER 32

Ashton

I KICK the punching bag in front of me. Then I jump and strike the bag with my knee, followed by a fake kick that transforms into a punch mid-air.

Where the fuck is Marcus?

I made the usual arrangements to ensure the gym is empty while all that's required of his billionaire majesty is to show up and let me work off some of my angry energy… using his face.

Once I've let off some steam, I plan on stopping by Kendall's apartment so I can undo what I did by leaving in anger. And once that's done, I'll reason with her—and by reason, I mean find some non-barbarian way to explain to her that she's mine and that I intend to keep her, no matter how many times she ghosts me and denies our relationship.

The door creaks.

"Fucking finally." I turn to face Marcus and freeze.

The person wearing all the usual gear is not my friend.

No. It's Kendall, and she makes me realize that fighting accoutrements like gloves, shin guards, and especially foot pads, can be sexy as hell when worn by the right person.

"Hi," she says, her speech slurred by the mouthguard.

"Hey." I spit mine out. "What are you doing here?"

She walks up to me and raises her gloves. "I came to apologize and to let you hit me, if that's what it takes to earn your forgiveness."

I stare at her, equal parts stunned and offended. "I'd never hit you. Not even if you were about to murder me."

"Oh." Looking disappointed, she spits out her mouthguard. "Then you'll have to forgive me without any violence." Mirroring actions to words, she lowers her gloves. "And... I'm sorry I thought you were that Ash-hole. Also, I should have told you about Candy Berlin. Most importantly, I'm sorry I didn't see us as a couple. I should have. I was just worried that you'd break up with me when you learned about my side business."

I rip my gloves off so I can grip her arms. "How could you think that?"

Her chin quivers slightly. "You told me you wouldn't date me if I were a sex worker."

"I said that I would have a problem with your job. Big difference."

Her eyes brighten. "Oh."

"Now, if that's the full extent of your apology, I officially forgive you. Also, I shouldn't have told you to go home to New York by yourself. I was just upset with my sister getting sick, and the revelations, but I swear I was going to go over to your place after this session and—"

She rises on tiptoes and silences me with a kiss.

I return it with savage satisfaction, nibbling on her lip as I do.

She moans and bites my lip—hard.

I rip the gear off my body and toss it in every direction, finishing with the groin protector—the lack of which my rock-hard cock appreciates. Then I tear away her outfit, all without breaking the rough kiss.

Once all she's wearing are the foot pads, I splay her on the mat, peel the pads from her feet, and glide my hands over the elegantly curved arches. "These are mine," I inform her hoarsely. "No one is going to look at them. Not if—"

"Umm, I thought we—"

"I mean it," I growl. "I will end any man who so much as looks at these feet."

She dampens her kiss-swollen lips. "Can we put a pin in that? We can return to this topic later."

"Fucking fine." Focusing on her right foot, I drag my tongue from her big toe over the arch and bite her heel. I then glide my tongue down her calf and over the inside of her creamy thigh until I reach her pussy— where I feast like I'm starving. Which I am.

"Holy fuck, I'm coming," she cries out and buckles under me, her elegant toes curling.

"You will come again for me," I decree as I enter her soft, snug, and oh-so-wet-for-me pussy.

Her nails score my back.

I piston into her, channeling all that unspent energy into the act.

She screams my name, digs her nails deeper, and comes, her inner walls squeezing me with such intensity that my own release explodes into her and my vision goes starry, as if someone has punched me in the face but in the best possible way.

Afterward, we lie on our sides, faces toward each other, limbs intertwined.

As I look at her, something swells in my chest. A realization that might be much too soon to share with her, but I—

"You know," she says, her voice languid. "If MMA sparring is always like this, I will permanently replace Marcus."

Ah. I didn't even bother to think about Marcus's role in this, but in hindsight, she must've arranged this swap with him via Emma.

"Listen, fashionista..." I take her hand in mine. My heart thumps heavily in my chest. "There's something serious I want to talk to you about."

She nods. "I know. And my answer is yes. I will move in with you."

I stare at her. "How did you—oh, never mind. I didn't realize Marcus was a fucking gossip."

She shrugs. "He and Emma are married now. Whatever you tell one, you're telling the other."

"Noted." I squeeze her hand gently. "But that wasn't actually what I wanted to say."

She sighs theatrically. "Fine. You win. With us moving in together and VersaWear on the horizon, I guess I can kill Candy Berlin." She nods at our scattered gear. "You've made some compelling arguments. But I really love to wear open-toe shoes. And sandals. And peep-toe shoes. And—"

"I get it." With me around, I doubt anyone will be so foolish as to risk their balls by staring at her feet, so what she wears isn't all that critical. "But what I wanted to say was something else."

"Oh. What then?"

I interlace my fingers with hers and take a deep breath. It might be too soon, but I feel compelled to tell her. "That day when you fell into my arms, I started to fall for you."

Her eyes go wide. "You did?"

"I did. And now I'm all the way fallen. As in…" I bring her hand to my lips and kiss it tenderly. "I love you."

A huge smile lights her face, turning her beauty incandescent. Unlacing our fingers, she pulls me closer, until her lips are brushing my earlobe. "I love you too," she whispers. "And I want to be with you. Date you. Be your girlfriend. Even if it means I'll have to wear Crocs. Or even UGGs."

We kiss then and make love, this time gently,

mindfully, punctuating the words we've spoken with our bodies. And when we're lying there, spent, I have to admit that Kendall was right.

MMA sessions with her are far, far superior to those with Marcus.

Epilogue

KENDALL

SQUEAK.

Squeak.

Squeak.

No, these are not the proverbial wheels that get the grease. It's the sound of my bad idea. I figured if I'm using fitness celebs instead of models in this fashion show, why not have them wear sneakers? Turns out, rubber soles plus the vinyl floor of the runway equals ear torture.

I run over to the DJ, take a microphone, and tell him to crank up the music—a remix of an old recording my parents kept, one that features yours truly in a marching band. (Hey, it's my show, and I do what I want to.) As I hoped, the sounds of the sousaphone muffle the squeaking, and for all I know, that may be what it was invented for.

Returning to the stage, I stand next to Ashton and examine the crowd.

Anyone who is anyone has come to see the VersaWear 2.0 show—and not just because of how popular the original VersaWear is. No, as usual, I can thank my fitness mogul boyfriend. He's clearly pulled some strings. Also, and surprisingly, some of the people from the fashion world are here at Tierre's behest. As soon as VersaWear became a hit, Mr. Former Boss started telling anyone who would listen that I was always his protégée, so is it any wonder I'm as good as I am?

"This part is a little surprise," Ashton whispers. "One that I helped with."

Uh-oh. I'm not sure I want any more surprises.

Too late. The more muscular of the models does a backflip—not ripping her outfit in the process, which is a win that I'll take. The problem is, she loses her balance and falls onto the woman behind her, who dominoes into the one behind her, and so on until there's an orgy of windmilling models in a heap on the runway.

To my shock, the audience claps, enthusiastically.

I guess they thought it was all carefully choreographed. I mean, such a clusterfuck couldn't happen by accident, right?

I make sure my mic is on mute before I hiss at Ashton, "Any more surprises I should know of?"

As if to answer, one of the models gets back on her feet, pulls out a jump rope, and hops down the runway over said rope like a demented bunny.

Again, the crowd applauds.

"I didn't know about that one," Ashton whispers.

Another model starts doing pushups, and the one next to her, burpees—a word that should have no place in the world of high fashion.

"I didn't know about that either," Ashton says before the crowd applauds yet again.

By the time the models leave the runway, I sprout at least a couple of gray hairs, but luckily, given everyone's reactions thus far, it's a success.

Now for the dramatic finish... I clutch the microphone tightly and get on the runway, where I face the crowd and give a thank-you speech.

"And last but not least," I say toward the end. "I want to thank the love of my life, Ashton Vancroft." I gesture to where he's standing and do a come-hither gesture. "Please, come join me."

Ashton looks confused—and it serves him right.

When he's standing next to me, I whisper, "Not so fun when you're the subject of a surprise, is it?"

The confusion is replaced with a cocky grin. "Bring it on."

Okay. He asked for it.

"To end the festivities, there's something that I wanted to do *in front of everyone*." I stick my hand into my pocket and clutch a small box. Bending my knee, I look up at Ashton—whose eyes are now the size of quarters—and solemnly say, "So far, you've done all the firsts. You were the first to realize we were serious. The first to ask me to move in together, and the first to say,

'I love you.' Today, I wanted to be the first at something. So, Ashton Vancroft, will you make me the happiest woman in the world by marrying me?"

The people around us seem to collectively hold their breath.

Ashton's eyes gleam. "Yes. But can you do me a favor first?"

"Name it."

"Stand up for a second."

I do as he says.

To my shock, he pulls out a ring box from his pocket and gets on one knee. "I've been carrying this around, looking for a great opportunity to propose to you. It's been difficult to come up with something so special that it is worthy of how I feel about you. So, thank you from the bottom of my heart for setting up *this*. Now, considering I said yes, will you marry me?" He takes his ring out and slides it on my trembling finger.

"Yes," I gasp into the microphone.

The clapping that ensues is deafening—as is the joyous beating of my heart.

He said yes.

And I did too.

I'm going to marry Ashton Vancroft, the man who's become my everything.

Our wedding will be fucking epic, but not as epic as our life together that will follow. Seventy years from now, when we're old and gray, our great-grandchildren may ask how they, too, can meet their soulmate. And I'll tell them what I know:

Fly off a treadmill and then hold on tight.

The right person will always be there to catch you.

Sneak Peeks

Thank you for participating in Kendall and Ashton's journey!

Ready for another steamy, laugh-out-loud, feel-good romance? Read *Billionaire Grump*, the story of a Rome-obsessed billionaire with attitude, a quirky, sweet plant lover, and a meet cute gone very wrong...or very right?

Love a trip to the Sunshine State? Read *Billionaire Surfer*! It follows Brooklyn, an overworked single mom in desperate need of a vacation, and Evan, a billionaire surfer who, like the ocean waves, might just sweep Brooklyn off of her feet.

To make sure you never miss a release, sign up for Misha's newsletter at www.mishabell.com and Anna's at www.annazaires.com.

Turn the page to read previews from *Billionaire Grump* and *Billionaire Surfer*!

Excerpt from Billionaire Grump

BY MISHA BELL

Juno

When I'm late for a job interview and get stuck on an elevator with an annoyingly sexy, Ancient Rome-obsessed grump, the last thing I expect is for him to be the billionaire owner of the building. I also don't expect to almost kill him... accidentally, of course.

Sure, I don't get the plant care position I applied for, but I do receive an interesting offer.

Lucius needs to trick the public (and his grandma) into thinking he's in a relationship, and I need tuition money to get my botany degree. Our arrangement is mutually beneficial—that is, until I start catching feelings.

If being a cactus lover has taught me anything, it's that

if you get too close, there's a good chance you'll end up hurt.

Lucius

Post-elevator incident, I'm left with three things: my favorite water bottle full of pee, a life threatening allergic reaction, and paparazzi photos of my "girlfriend" and I that make my Gram the happiest woman alive.

Naturally, my next step is to blackmail—I mean, convince—this (admittedly cute) girl to pretend to date me. That way, my grandma stays happy, and as a bonus, I can keep the gold diggers at bay.

Unfortunately, my arch nemesis, a.k.a. biology, kicks in, and the whole "not getting physical" part of our agreement becomes increasingly hard to abide by. Worse yet, the longer I'm with Juno, the more my delicately crafted icy exterior melts away.

If I'm not careful, Juno will tear down my walls completely.

———

"Are you calling me stupid?" I snap. Anyone could have trouble with these damn buttons, not just a person with dyslexia.

He looks pointedly at the buttons. "Stupid is as stupid does."

I grind my teeth, painfully. "You're an asshole. And you've watched *Forrest Gump* one too many times."

His lips flatten. "That movie wasn't the origin of that saying. It's from Latin: *Stultus est sicut stultus facit.*"

I roll my eyes. "What kind of pretentious *stultus* quotes Latin?"

The steel in his eyes is so cold I bet my tongue would get stuck if I tried to lick his eyeball. "I don't know. Maybe the 'idiot' who happens to like everything related to Rome, including their numerals."

My jaw drops open. "You made this decision?" I wave toward the elevator buttons.

He nods.

Shit. He probably heard me earlier, which means I started the insults. In my defense, he did make an idiotic choice.

I exhale a frustrated breath. "If you're such an expert on Roman numerals, you could've told me which one to press."

He crosses his arms over his chest. "You didn't ask me."

My hackles rise again. "Ask you? You looked like you might bite my head off for just existing."

"That's because you delayed—"

The elevator jerks to a stop, and the lights around us dim.

We both stare at the doors.

They stay shut.

He turns to me and narrows his eyes accusingly. "What did you press now?"

"Me? How? I've been facing you. Unfortunately."

With an annoying headshake, he stalks toward the panel with the buttons, and I have to leap away before I get trampled.

"You probably pressed something earlier," he mutters. "Why else would we be stuck?"

Why is it illegal to choke people? Just a few seconds with my hands on his throat would be a calming exercise.

Instead, I glare at his back, which is blocking my view of what he's doing, if anything. "The poor elevator probably just committed suicide over these Roman numerals. It knew that when someone sees things like L and XL, they think of T-shirt sizes for Neanderthal types like you. And don't get me started on that XXX button, which is a clear reference to porn. It creates a hostile work env—"

"Can you shut up so I can get us out of this?" he snaps.

His words bring home the reality of our situation: it's been over a minute, and the doors are still closed.

Dear saguaro, am I really stuck here? With this guy? What about my interview?

"Silence, finally," he says with satisfaction and moves to the side, so I see him jam his finger at the "help" button.

"It's a miracle that's not in Latin," I can't help but say. "Or Klingon."

"Hello?" he says into the speaker under the button, his voice dripping with irritation.

No reply, not even static.

"Anyone there?" His annoyance is clearly rising to new heights. "I'm late for an important meeting."

"And I'm late for an interview," I chime in, in case it matters.

He pauses to arch a thick eyebrow at me. "An interview? For what position?"

I stand straighter. "I'm sure the likes of you don't realize this, but the plants in this building don't take care of themselves."

Wait. Have I said too much? Could he torpedo my interview—assuming this elevator snafu hasn't done it already? What does he do here, anyway—design ridiculous elevators? That can't be a full-time job, can it?

"A tree hugger," he mutters under his breath. "That tracks."

What an asshole. I've never hugged a tree in my life. I'm too busy talking to them.

He returns his scowling attention to the "help" button—though now I'm thinking it should've been labeled as "no help."

"Hello? Can you hear me?" he shouts. "Answer now, or you're fired."

I roll my eyes. "Is it a good idea to be a dick to the person who can save us?"

He blows out an audible breath. "It doesn't matter..

The button must be malfunctioning. They wouldn't dare ignore me."

I pull out my trusty phone, a nice and simple Nokia 3310. "Full of yourself much?"

He stares at my hands incredulously. "So that's why the elevator got stuck. It went through a time warp and transported us to 2008."

I frown at the lack of reception on my Nokia. "This version was released in 2017."

"It still looks dumber than a brain-dead crash test dummy." He proudly pulls an iPhone from his pocket. "*This* is what a phone should look like."

I scoff. "That's what constant distraction looks like. Anyway, if your iNotSoSmartPhone—trademarked—is so great, it should have some reception, right?"

He glances at his screen, but I can tell he already knows the truth: no reception for his darling either.

Still, I can't resist. "See? Your genius of a phone is just as useless. All it's good for is turning people into social-media-checking zombies."

He hides the device, like a protective parent. "On top of all your endearing qualities, you're a technophobe too?"

I debate throwing my Nokia at his head but decide it's not worth shelling out sixty-five bucks for a replacement. "Just because I don't want to be distracted doesn't mean I'm a technophobe."

"Actually, my phone is great at blocking out distractions." He puts the headphones back over his ears. "See?" He presses play, and I hear the faint riffs of heavy metal.

"Very mature," I mouth at him.

"Sorry," he says overly loudly. "I can't hear any distractions."

Fine. Whatever. At least he has good taste in music. My cactus and I are big fans of Metallica, which is what I think he's listening to.

I begin to pace back and forth.

I'm stuck, and I'm late. If this elevator jam doesn't resolve itself in the next minute or two, I can pretty much kiss the new job goodbye—and by extension, my tuition money. No tuition money means no botany degree, which has been my dream for the last few years.

By saguaro's juices, this sucks really bad.

I sneak a glance at the hottie—I mean, asshole.

What would he say about someone with dyslexia wanting a college degree? Probably that I'd need a university that uses coloring books. In truth, even coloring books wouldn't help that much—I can never stay inside those stupid lines.

I sigh and look away, increasingly worried. My dreams aside, what if the elevator stays stuck for a while?

The most immediate problem is my growing need to pee—but paradoxically, a longer-term worry will be finding liquids to drink.

I wonder... If you're thirsty enough, does your body reabsorb the water from the bladder? Also, could I

MacGyver a filter to reclaim the water in my urine with what I have on me? Maybe through cat hair?

I shiver, and only partially from the insane AC that's somehow reaching me even in here. In the short term, it would be so much better if it were hot instead of cold. I'd sweat out the liquids and not need to pee, though I guess I'd die of thirst sooner. I sneak an envious glance at the large stranger. I bet he has a bladder the size of a blimp. He also has a stainless-steel bottle that's probably filled with water that he likely won't share.

There's also the question of food. I don't have anything edible with me, apart from a can of cat food... and, theoretically, the cat herself.

No. I'd sooner eat this stranger than poor Atonic.

As if psychic, the stranger's stomach growls.

Crap. With this guy being so big and mean, he'd probably eat the cat. After that, he'd eat me... and not in a fun way.

I'm so, so screwed.

———

Visit www.mishabell.com to order your copy of *Billionaire Grump* today!

Excerpt from Billionaire Surfer

BY MISHA BELL

An overworked single mom from New York City. A billionaire surfer from Florida. Can the turn of the tide bring these two together?

Brooklyn

Ah, finally a vacation. My son is at summer camp. My worries are back in the city. Now I just get to sit back, relax, and... get into a heated argument with my Airbnb host? Speaking of heat, is the Florida sun getting to my head, or is it the drop-dead gorgeous man in front me?

My friends did say I need some *Vitamin D*...

But my life is complicated, and no amount of adventure-filled treasure hunting, steamy make-out sessions, or ocean-deep conversations can convince me that our beach affair could last. Especially once Evan learns my secret.

Evan

I'm rich on paper, but I don't live my life like a typical billionaire. Nor do I date tourists. Especially ones who mistake me for a plumber and eat my breakfast before I have a chance to quell my hanger.

Brooklyn is argumentative, rude, stubborn, beautiful, smart, fun... Okay, let's say I kind of like her. That doesn't change the fact that she's only here for a week —or that I haven't told her an important fact about myself.

But if surfing has taught me anything, it's that you have to seize the moment before it's gone. And what if I don't want to let her go?

———

On the flight to Jacksonville, Reagan plays his video game while I do my best not to snap at him or any other innocent bystanders. Thanks to my shit luck, the Red Wedding arrived mere hours ago, giving me the kind of cramps that, if you gave them to a prisoner of war, would go against the Geneva Conventions.

Thanks, body. Was a relaxing plane ride too much to ask for?

I glare at my wrist where my birthday gift from last year resides. It's an Octothorpe Glorp, a fitness tracker that's supposed to warn me when Aunt Flo is coming to town. Often, I imagine the gizmo talking back to me in a voice that's a mix of Richard Simmons and Gollum:

My dear Precious, if I could, I'd keep every tampon you've ever used in a shrine and glue to them the smiles I cut out of my favorite pictures of you. Alas, when it comes to the feature you mention, I merely track your cycles, not predict them.

I suffer the rest of the flight as stoically as I can. Once we land, I rent a car and drive Reagan straight to the camp—a beachy and chill establishment that plays Jimmy Buffett on a loop.

"Okay, bye," Reagan says without a second of hesitation before running off to check the place out.

I wait to make sure he doesn't run back and tell me he doesn't like what he sees. Nope. He probably thinks I've already left, or has forgotten that I exist altogether.

"He'll have access to a phone," the nearest Boy-Scout-looking counselor says to me reassuringly. "And we have your number on file. Once he's settled in, he'll give you a call. Go."

With a sigh, I head back to the car and start driving.

My mood was already crummy, but now it's worse than that of a stressed-out, sleep-deprived, and tick-riddled hippopotamus. The green and idyllic nature around me only makes me feel shitty about where I actually live, as do the much nicer roads and cleaner streets. But then I almost run over an-honest-to-goodness live alligator and feel a little better about the comparison between my namesake in NYC and Palm Islet, Florida, the illustrious little town where my vacation is to be. Same goes when a deer tries to commit suicide by car a few minutes later, and when the woman in the car in front of me stops to rescue a turtle—getting peed on in the process.

Got to love Florida.

My Airbnb turns out to be located in a gated community, and the female security guard at the entrance is as thorough as a TSA officer. When all my papers seem to be in order, she wrinkles her nose and mutters something about the HOA usually prohibiting Airbnb rentals in the community, and that mine is a rare exception to the rule. She further informs me that the HOA usually charges an overnight guest fee, but that the owner of *my* Airbnb is exempt from "all the rules."

Oh, the humanity. How do the poor members of the HOA sleep at night? As I drive away, it takes effort not to ask if the HOA in this case stands for Hilariously Overbearing Authority.

Driving through the community, I notice that the houses are charming mixes of Spanish, Mediterranean, and Caribbean styles, and that they all have impeccable lawns—must be the same HOA ruling with an iron fist. But when I pull into the cul-de-sac where my Airbnb is located, the monotone pattern is broken. Houses number four and five on Gatorview Drive are twins, and both have sharp corners, are covered in mirrored surfaces and tons of chrome, and remind me of something you might see in a modern art museum.

Since one of these is mine, I assume both belong to the same HOA rules-exempt owner.

My mood lifts minutely as I spot the lake adjacent to both houses, with untouched nature on the opposite bank. The view from my Airbnb must be spectacular, though slightly less so than from the neighboring house.

I check my fitness tracker for the time.

Dearest Precious ought to consider taking more steps, to tighten those succulent thighs for my stalking—I mean viewing—pleasure.

Crap. I'm too early for check in, and it's getting pretty hot. According to Evan, who's been sending me taciturn texts on behalf of this Airbnb, the code for the garage lock can only be used after eleven-thirty, but I may die of heatstroke by then.

Also, I kind of want the vacation to start, along with the associated relaxation.

Why don't I test said code now?

Walking up to the garage, I type in the code and the door opens. Score! Between this and the lack of a car in the driveway or in the garage, I'm pretty sure I can get inside the house.

After parking in the garage, I open the door to the house proper—which, according to Evan, is the entrance I'll use to come and go.

The door leads right into an ultra-modern kitchen the size of my whole apartment, and there, on the granite island, stands a spread of yummy tapas.

Now this is a fancy welcome. I spot a tiny piece of

grilled salmon, a giant bean, a side of rice, an assortment of pickles, a ton of tiny vegetable plates, and something that looks and smells just like miso soup.

Japanese tapas?

Shrugging, I taste the salmon as I take in the lake view through a floor-to-ceiling window.

I'm jealous of Floridians yet again. In New York, you'd have to be a billionaire to have anything close to this house with this kind of view.

The fish is divine, so I sample each of the veggies, which are also amazing. Even the bean is tasty, and the miso soup is the best of its kind, sweet and savory in equal measure.

Suddenly, I hear rustling on the other side of the island.

What the hell?

The island is blocking my view, so I gingerly step over to where the sound is coming from—a sink that I couldn't see earlier.

I gasp.

A man is getting to his feet. Based on the tools scattered on the floor, I assume he must be a plumber here to fix said sink.

Now I'll admit, until today, if I were forced to picture a plumber in my head, he (is that sexist?) would look like Super Mario with a cartoonish mustache, coveralls, and as much sex appeal as a blobfish.

This plumber, however, has to be the hottest man I've ever seen.

His eyes are the clear blue of a Siberian Husky, his hair is the sun-bleached shade of a Golden Retriever's coat, and his sharp angular facial features are godlike with no dog analogs. Sadly, his ears are covered by headphones, but I bet they are sexy too. Oh, and his bare chest boasts an army of glistening muscles that include a six pack. Also, his nipples are hard.

Correction, it's *my* nipples that are hard.

Spotting me, he frowns, but he makes even grumpy look good. Then his gaze falls on what remains of the tapas, and his eyes beam icicles at me.

"Who are you?" he demands in a low growl that somehow manages to be sexy. "And why did you eat my fucking breakfast?"

———

Visit www.mishabell.com to order your copy of *Billionaire Surfer* today!